# BEGGING FOR IT

# BEGGING FOR IT
## EROTIC FANTASIES FOR WOMEN

EDITED BY
RACHEL KRAMER BUSSEL

Published in the United States by Cleis Press, an imprint of Start Midnight, LLC, 101 Hudson St, Suite 3705, Jersey City, NJ 07302.

Printed in the United States.
Cover design: Scott Idleman/Blink
Cover photograph: iStock
Text design: Frank Wiedemann
First Edition.
10 9 8 7 6 5 4 3 2 1

Trade paper ISBN: 978-1-62778-166-4
E-book ISBN: 978-1-62778-167-1

Parts of "*Babes*" by Elizabeth Black appear in her novel *No Restraint* (Xcite Books).

# Contents

# INTRODUCTION: BEGGARS *AND* CHOOSERS

Judging from the title *Begging for It*, you might picture women with their tongues hanging out, perhaps a little drool pooling on their lips, come-hither eyes, kneeling, breasts thrust forward, ripe and ready and eager. And you'd be right—but not entirely right.

The women you'll meet in this book manage to beg in all sorts of ways—boldly, silently, sweetly, submissively, nastily, hungrily. Sometimes, their begging is quite ardent, clear as a whistle, but other times, they may not even know what it is they're begging for. Each of them, though, is on a journey, a path to find something that's missing from her life at the start. Some are searching for a lover—or more than one—while others have a partner in lust but are still seeking a bit of magic, daring, adventure, to lure them somewhere they've been longing—begging—to go, if only in their dreams.

For this anthology, I wanted stories that spoke to the many ways fantasies can play out in our lives. I wanted femme fatales and shy, unsure women, those who have glimpsed their truest desires briefly but have yet to fully indulge them. I wanted the kind of women whose sexual energy radiates off of them, the kind who turn heads no matter what they're doing, the kind who look just-been-fucked—or just-fucked-someone—whether they actually have or not.

What I got were women who do indeed know what they want, whether it's rope bondage or humiliation, a corset or an erotic adventure, robots or rough sex, but who are also open to finding unexpected, incredible pleasure they could not have imagined. They're women on a mission, but they never know where exactly those missions will lead, and to me, that's the best part of sex, and erotica: that each time might wow us anew. When Lauren Marie Fleming writes, "I was wet, so wet I thought I'd drip on the floor, and my nipples were as hard as my clit, both threatening to make me come with the slightest touch," I'm right there with her, as Tabitha discovers what suspension can truly do for her, not to mention sexy Caleb.

These lusty ladies fall for cowboys, bosses, drag queens, rope wranglers, threesomes, Sirs and strangers, yet they never lose sight of that inner spark that has pushed them to say yes. In giving themselves to the objects of their affection, they're gaining something equally valuable. Sometimes, there's a different kind of give and take involved, such as with the masseuse in D. L. King's "A Proven Therapeutic Fact," who makes the delivery of a spanking a very special event.

These women are both begging and demanding, but most importantly, discovering the thrill of the unexpected. They are all sexual adventurers daring to go where they've never been before, or have only been in their dreams.

Rachel Kramer Bussel
Atlantic City, New Jersey

# SYMPHONY

## Dena Hankins

She settles deeper into the piled pillows, their crisp white covers rustling against her naked shoulders. Her soft exhalation, almost inaudible to her, stimulates the delicate wireless electrodes adhered to her cheeks, throat, chest and belly. The signal is transmitted to the listeners and sets off a fast scritching from the dark edge of the room.

*You weren't joking about getting readings almost immediately. The sound level meter is working.*

*Do you think the condenser mic is close enough? That didn't read.*

A sterile light, reminiscent of the dentist's office, glares off the sheet. She keeps her eyes closed against the brightness but wants to feel it on her bare skin. She's allowed to have as much or as little covering her as she likes.

*Haven't seen you since that Psychoacoustics conference. Still focusing on Systematic Musicology?*

*Yep. They brought me in for my expertise with fractional octave filters.*

She slides the sheet down to her belly, revealing herself to the analytical gaze of the shadowed musicologists. She strokes the sides of her breasts, cups them in her hands, lifts and squeezes them. Her inhaled breath whistles between pursed lips. At the top of the breath, she pinches both nipples, squeezing and holding. The breath leaves her nose on a whimper and she hears a clipboard tap someone's wristwatch.

*So we're really doing this. Doesn't it feel...sordid...in front of all these people?*

*If we can use what we learn to trigger sympathetic neurological and biological effects in listeners, we should feel honored.*

*Music that can make people...come.*

*I hope she doesn't overdo it. It won't work if she's just acting.*

The palpable focus turns up her sensitivity and she sends one cold hand stroking over her ribs. Her semi-reclining position mounds her belly and encourages the folds above and below. They watch and listen and she whines her anticipation for them. Yes, she wants to turn herself on, to roll up the sunny hill of pleasure and play on the craggy peaks of joy that will send her home to herself, triumphant.

This is best done bare. She kicks the top sheet off altogether and slits her eyes to look down her body.

She feels her nudity more acutely in the shadows than in the light.

*Alto sax here.*

*We're using A-frequency-weighting on the SLM, right?*

She swipes two fingers of lube from the stainless-steel dish they had provided and slicks it into the folds of her labia. Her fingertip nudges her tender clit, eliciting a chattering chirp, and she presses the flat of her fingers to either side with a croon.

*Not too fast. Can't have the symphony last only a minute or two.*

She leaves her hand there and moves her other hand to the

swell of her belly and the spongy flesh protecting her pubic bone. Her palm, leathery and calloused from constructing, tuning and playing drums, catches on the springy hairs with a soft rasp. The gentle pull has her swallowing with a gulp.

Was that sound sexy? She doubts herself suddenly, for the first time. She squeezes her eyes closed. These noises, so raw and unfiltered in the ears of colleagues and acquaintances and friends, reveal her arousal. Naked on a starched white sheet, she struggles with silence, knowing that any sound will bare her need more deeply than the light, the space, the avid eyes. She could jerk off for them and feel private if she hadn't agreed to give them her sounds.

*Cough. Rustle.*

*Shhh.*

No wrong way.

Stretching her back, pushing out her belly, she makes room for air. She drinks it, sizzling, between her teeth and lets it rumble in her chest and throat on the way out. She stretches the tight muscles of her jaw, dropping her mouth wide open, and the next breath comes out as a groan.

*Oboe. She has the timbre and sustain of woodwinds.*

Breathing has put her back in her body and she opens her eyes. The tight focus of the light ends just below her diaphragm, above her belly button. Below that is a hint of light, the reflection from her skin and the bright sheet, bronzing her crinkly hair and texturizing the shadows between her drawn-together thighs.

Looking, she touches her clit with two fingers. A husky throat-clearing from a watcher surprises a jangly laugh from her. The observer effect. She feels her clit swell in the valley between her fingers and shifts them in minuscule circles, gurgles flowing from her throat.

*We can try trombone for matching these harmonics.*

She modulates the pressure of her fingers and starts to gnaw at her sounds, little yelps trading air with purrs. The tension in her builds and her lungs fill and empty more and more insistently, the tangy hum alternating with gasping and squeaking.

*Violin and cello trading off, perhaps?*

Too good to stop but not enough for the ear-shattering release she wants to give them. She concentrates her circles right down on the head of her clit, holding her clit-hood back with her other hand, and lets herself caterwaul with the delicious excitement of an intermediate come during an extended sexual playtime.

*Horns and cymbals, I think.*

*She's not using the semitone scale. Oh boy, this is going to be fun.*

Her jerking body makes every chuckle a polyphonic lava burst. Joy erupts from her in babbling laughter as she engages all the muscles in her torso in service of the orgasm. She tosses her head back and jerks it forward with each hard-wringing wave of abdominal strength, her chortles shifting to a warbling, trilling scream.

*I'm hearing flute, don't you think?*

*The dial on the quasi-peak program meter is dancing. Really. Look!*

Gasping, panting syllables pour senselessly from her mouth as she trembles. They gain depth and turn rough when she pushes the dildo into her fluttering pussy. Her hot, velvety flesh massages the insensitive tool, grasping and pulling, creating a direct line from her vocal cords to her sexual center. Bleats turn to hoots turn to a ragged roar as she fucks herself roughly, pounding the base against all the tenderness outside while rubbing and pushing so far up inside that she chokes finally on sobbing snarls. Hiccups put dead stop *thunks* between grinding ragged croaks.

*I...fuck...*

*I'm seeing spurious tones at double and triple her base frequency. Her harmonic distortion is glorious.*

She slows her thrusting and then leaves the dildo hot inside her pussy. An easy moan mirrors the long undulations still sweeping her muscles. She turns on her side, feeling the electrodes shift with her breasts, and reaches around to touch her asshole. The dry pull reminds her of the lube and she scoops up a liberal amount.

*Is that her heart? This movement will begin with throbbing tympani.*

*That makes sense emotionally, but let's see what the equal-loudness contours show.*

She thinks briefly of the careful setup, the precise placement of the piezoelectric and condenser mics, but goes with her own desire. Leaving the dildo aside, she slips off the edge of the bed and leans against it, her belly a wonderful prop for her torso. Both hands behind her, she pulls her cheeks apart and slathers her asshole with lube. She sighs as the fingertips of both hands tease the quickly softening folds. The hard light shows every freckle on her chest and glares on her nipple rings, but the electrodes absorb all frequencies. The weight on her belly forces her to breathe in with greater force, so she alternates powerful inhalation with a slow drone.

*Um...harmonium...and tabla...you can see the rhythm on the meter.*

As her asshole heats and eases, she presses inward. She finds the horribly, deliciously balanced place, not thrusting but pulsating...

*Oh...that slow, low sax.*

...only withdrawing in order to slide back in...

*How many rattles can one throat produce?*

...adding fingers for the stretch...

*Her sustain is incredible.*

She grabs the dildo, lubes it until it's dripping, and turns around. Holding its flared base against the mattress, she backs onto it, forcing it past the constriction of her sphincters with the power of her weight.

From groan to scream, she rips her throat open the way the dildo tears into her ass. The messy, dense, gnarled sensation translates as sound too complicated to analyze in a single hearing and she knows that the not painful forced feeling will challenge their best ears, their wisest and most widely experienced experts.

*Are we getting this? We're still recording, right?*

*Um, yes. Of course. I mean...fuck...I hope we got that. All the dials are twitching.*

She uses the mattress to hold the dildo deep in her ass and arrows her hands into her pussy. Her arms curve around the pendant mass of her belly, hanging out and down and making room for all the air in the room to fill her lungs and be reborn as aural sex.

Spreading the sculptural labia, pulling back the clit-hood, she grunts with the urge to thrust her hard clit into some soft, receptive orifice. She wants to fuck with it and jacks it off with thumb and curled index finger. She pushes her hips forward into her grasping fingers and screeches at the near-loss of the dildo in her ass. She thrusts back onto it and then rebounds, the beginning of a hard bounce that shoves her hips around in an orgy between her hands and her cock and her pussy and her ass and her clit and her pussy and her ass and her cock.

*Unh...unh...god, yes...keep going...you can take more...*

Shifting her legs farther apart, she transmutes the quivering exhaustion in her thighs into motivation, layering the pain and fear of collapse over her emotional fear that she will come apart this time, that no one can go this far and reassemble as a single human entity.

She is no longer able to maintain a regular rhythm and her slurping, smacking yelps and retching, grinding howls inundate the room.

*Oh…fuck…can I…yes, like that…*

*She's in the red zone…oh, more tongue…I gotta monitor the…*

She shoves her pungent knuckles in her mouth, tasting herself—she is musky and briny and peppery. The muffling of her voice allows thought to reassert itself and she realizes that it's time to give her body a rest—at least the muscles of her legs.

*Wh-what happened? Is she done? D-don't stop. Please.*

*Shh. Compression and intensity have increased though volume has decreased.*

She puts a hand on the dildo in her ass and rolls onto the bed. Lying flat, she props her heel on the base of the dildo to keep it in place and presses her pussy with the flat of her hand. Her palm is softened with lube but still decorated with thick calluses in ridges and pads.

When she pulls on her labia, twisting and pinching, her tongue taps the roof of her mouth. When she rubs tenderized, sore tissues, her moan is both pure and deep, an expression of love for herself. She cradles her clit in its hood and rocks it gently back and forth, subtly stroking it.

*She's gone within now. So quiet, but not silent. Remember this fulgent, brimming, congested, saturated precipice. The last movement comes from this place.*

Without changing her oblique touch, her heart thumps hard, once, twice, wringing gasps each time. She plummets, free-falling without fear because there is no ground.

She crows with triumph and throws her shoulders back, her fingers scrambling to stay with her clit. The dildo shoves out so hard that it folds between her heel and her asshole, her continued cheers changing into a circular melody that slowly, over minutes, devolves into sobs, each with its own shadow attached.

As her breathing slows and her heart eases, her sobs turn into humming. She straightens her leg and rests her hands on the expanse of her belly. Each breath in recoups energy, redefines the integrity of her body, while each breath out holds a language and song of its own.

*Wait. Wait for it.*

After long moments, she opens her eyes to the glare of the light. Blinded, one last gusty sigh catches in her throat and trembles on the needle of the vibration analyzer.

*Beautiful.*

# TABITHA
# THE CAT

## Lauren Marie Fleming

The fog rolled up my fishnets, like a nervous lover, cold and clammy, exploring my crevices. I shivered, and opened the blacked-out door, heading into the darkness.

A velvet curtain stood between my world and his, and I hesitated for a moment, like a girl on the first day of college, savoring the moment before her whole life changed. Pulling the curtain aside, I stepped toward my destiny.

"Welcome!" a shockingly perky girl shouted, greeting me with a bright, white smile that contrasted with the dark walls surrounding her. She had on a pink tutu, black bodice and glittery purple wings.

"Hi," I squeaked in response, my nerves getting the best of me.

"Aw, are you a newbie?" she questioned, handing me a form on a clipboard.

"Is it that obvious?" I asked, taking a pen from the bouquet on the small table in front of the fairy girl.

"Nah, well, yeah, but don't worry, being a newbie is good around these parts. Fresh meat. The boys will love ya."

"Sounds intense," I said, filling out my consent form and liability waiver.

"Only if you want it to be. We're strict on boundaries here, so don't feel like you need to do anything you're not comfortable doing. The only person you need to impress tonight is yourself," the girl said, sounding like the greeting card my mother got me for high school graduation.

I didn't come to this dungeon for motivation. As cute as the fairy was, my ideal type normally, she was not what I was looking for tonight. So I said my goodbyes and headed into the party.

"One last thing," the greeter said after me.

"Yes?" I asked, impatiently.

"What's your scene name?"

"Tabitha," I replied, closing the curtain and walking away.

She'd been my favorite cat as a kid, and I always admired the grace with which she twisted and curled, scratching her nails on her pole wrapped in rope. I hadn't planned on using Tabitha as a scene name—I didn't even know I needed a scene name until I was asked for one—but now Tabitha felt like home, a place I'd inhabited many times before.

Tonight, I was Tabitha the cat.

Slinking my way through the crowd, I tried not to look desperate as I searched for his familiar face. A sea of kink swirled around me, and I needed a rock on which to anchor myself. Caleb was to be my lifesaver, and distress set in when I could not find him in the dungeon depths.

"Hello there," a woman in white said, approaching me. "May I...ning?"

"What?" I asked, unable to hear her fully over the moans coming from a cage next to me.

"May I be of service to you this evening?" she asked, louder this time.

Suddenly, something hard and strong hit me from behind, jerking my head to the side, shoving a soft piece of cloth roughly into my throat. "She's mine tonight, Jade," a voice growled in my ear, sending fear and excitement shooting through my body.

The lights went out as a canvas bag was placed over my head, muting the world around me. Disappointment set in as I heard the clip of handcuffs on my wrists. *I told him rope*, I thought to myself. *I came here for rope.*

Caleb and I had met three weeks before at a found art show downtown, both of us fawning over the curvaceous master of the Western-themed sculptures, exquisitely executed statues featuring characters straight out of my hometown rodeo—clowns, bulls, broncos—all created out of hay, twine and rope.

I'd spotted him from across the room earlier in the night, black buzzed head, crisp button-up shirt, emerald-green tie and slacks, and hadn't been able to keep my eyes off of him since. He was extremely tall and very masculine, a shocking change from the short, feminine people to whom I usually found myself drawn, yet here I was, drooling over this well-dressed stranger.

"You like rope?" Caleb asked me as we stood next to each other in the line to meet the artist.

"No. I mean, maybe. I guess so. I don't know, why?" I asked, flustered by his question.

"Well," Caleb said, chuckling, "you're fondling that piece like a lover, so I just thought..."

Caleb's thought was interrupted by a forward movement in the line.

"Hello, welcome," the artist said, taking his hand and shaking it. I waited patiently for my turn with her, but was too distracted to ask any of the questions I'd had earlier. I simply gave my compliments and left.

Caleb was outside smoking a cigar, an act that usually

disgusts me but tonight I found myself aroused by the glowing ash. "Hello," I stammered, standing awkwardly in the doorway, not quite sure where to go once I left this space.

"Come over here," Caleb commanded, and I found myself gliding toward him, pulled by something beyond my own will.

"Get on your knees," he said sternly, and I fell for him. Instinctually, I opened my mouth and looked up, eager to take whatever this stranger wanted to give me.

"Stay," he commanded, leaning back against the wall and relaxedly smoking his cigar. In the moments that passed, I asked myself what I was doing there, on my knees, next to a busy street, destroying my tights, wind blowing my skirt up for the whole block to see. My girlfriend was waiting for me at the bar down the street, but here I was instead, obeying the will of a stranger.

"Stick out your tongue and curl it a bit," he said, and I did, enabling him to place a warm ball of ash in me. It sat there for a while, turning to mush, and I wondered if I was supposed to spit or swallow, but then he kissed me, and the taste of salty sulfur in my mouth mixed with sweet tobacco in his, and my whole body lit on fire.

"What's your name?" I asked, coming up for air.

"You can call me Caleb," he said, and handed me his card. "Come by my dungeon sometime."

The handcuffs were cold and tight but not wholly unpleasant. They weren't what I had come here for, but they were doing the trick, exciting me, inciting fear. Caleb pulled me by them for a ways and shoved me against something cold, hard and possibly glass. I could hear murmurs of people in the background, but I focused on the sound of Caleb breathing. We had negotiated a general idea of what the evening would look like over email, but I didn't want details. I wanted to be taken by Caleb, made to surrender to him, be bound to him.

And I wanted rope. I wanted lots and lots and lots of rope.

Rope was the only thing I'd been able to think about since meeting Caleb that night at the art show. I grew up around cowboys and vaqueros; rope was a part of my life early on, a thing both of function and show. I could lasso a plastic cow-head attached to a bail of hay by ten, a moving calf by twelve, but these days the closest thing I got to my cowgirl past was the gingham dress and braided pigtails I was wearing tonight, a dress I had bought just for this scene.

A dress I could feel Caleb unzipping right now. He ungagged me and uncuffed one hand, slipped my dress and bra straps off together in one stroke, and placed my arm by my side, repeating on the other side until I stood there wearing my fishnets, heels, a canvas bag over my head and nothing else. I felt a swell of vulnerability, exposed there for who-knows-how-many people, every freckle and scar, stretch mark and fat roll showing, nothing to hide behind. That swell turned into a tsunami of fear as I heard the unmistakable sound of rope pulled through gloves, a dry snake crunching through soft underbrush, ready to strike.

Caleb took a coil and ran it down my back, from the nape of my neck to the heel of my left foot, over and back up the right foot, circling around at my hips and scratching at my belly, bringing back sensations of childhood rope burn so clearly that I could almost smell the hay. *This*, I thought, relaxing my body, leaning into the large bulk of rope Caleb was now pressing against my front side, *this is what I came here for.*

Two large swaths of rope were placed on each of my shoulders, the weight of which felt comforting, like a hug from an old friend. Caleb pulled from each end of a coil on my right side and began wrapping them across my chest and around me, in a figure-eight motion, twisting and tying the ends around each other every time they met. His hands moved swiftly, and I could tell he had done this before. I, however, was in a brand-new place, one of submission and patience, two things at which I needed practice, apparently, as I fidgeted and slacked, making Caleb yank hard on the rope, putting me in my place. Soon, the rope bodice around my waist was so tight, I had no choice but to stand up straight and attentive.

Taking a second coil, Caleb began wrapping rope around my legs, tying cuffs on each ankle and eventually attaching them to rope cuffs he made around my thighs. I moaned as he pressed the rope against my fishnet-covered crotch and rubbed. I leaned my head back in pleasure and he yanked the rope on my chest, snapping it back up to attention for me. "I'm sorry," I said, speaking for the first time since we had started. "I'm new at this."

"That's no excuse for slacking," Caleb said sternly, pulling up my chin, pushing down my ass and correcting my posture. "I thought you were a lady. Act like one."

I've never been one for pleasing men, preferring instead to date women I could easily push around, but I found myself inexplicably attached to Caleb, my pleasure bound to his approval. *I will not move again*, I told myself, and stood there like a determined statue while Caleb began attaching my rope to something squeaky and metallic.

"Take a deep breath in," Caleb commanded, and as I did so I was lifted off the ground, my feet, arms and torso taking flight all at once. At first, I couldn't breathe, the wind knocked out of me by the force of levitation, but then gradually my body settled into the feeling of flight, and I began to appreciate the dual sensations of intense pressure and freeing weightlessness.

For the first time in my life, I let myself completely and totally surrender to the moment. Caleb was in charge. Of my body, of my mind, of my safety.

I didn't know how much time had gone by, but Caleb kept on tying, twist of rope after twist of rope, and all I could do was yield to his touch, my body limp, held up by his mastery. Finally, he came over and placed his hands on both sides of my face. "Are you ready?" he asked.

A nodded a meek yes, and he took the canvas sack off of my head, revealing my view of the dungeon from overhead. As my eyes adjusted to the light, I realized I was in the center of a small room that opened off of the larger dungeon and had floor-to-ceiling mirrors. Everywhere I looked, I saw myself, bright red-and-white rope contrasting against my olive skin, hair dangling feet above the ground. I looked graceful, catlike, an aerial ballerina about to pounce on a toy, except I was the toy, and Caleb was doing the pouncing tonight.

I never wanted this moment to end.

"Excuse me," I said, working up the courage to talk. "Um, excuse me, Sir?"

"Yes?" he responded curtly.

"Sir," I said, choosing my words carefully, "would you be so kind as to honor me with a photo of your stunning work?"

Caleb smiled, filling my being with happiness. His smile was sorcery on my soul, and I had caused that magic. I had pleased him.

"My phone is in my purse," I added, and he walked over to my pile of things, things someone apparently had brought from the place where he first grabbed and gagged me. A part of me fell in love with Caleb at that moment, seeing how well he had taken care of my things, and of me. My dress was neatly folded in the corner, my shoes and purse placed gently next to them. This was a man who understood the care fine apparel deserves.

I hung there, gracefully limp, completely bound to the shape and movement he had chosen for me, as he took photo after photo of every part of my body. Any self-consciousness I had felt before melted away with the salacious look of hunger on his face, his yearning and appreciation of my body wonderfully apparent. Again, I found myself excited by his happiness, proud of myself for being the cause.

When he grabbed me and kissed me, he standing straight and tall, me hanging face-to-face with his six-foot, six-inch self, I melted, letting go of every last bit of tension held in the most minute fascia in my body. I was wet, so wet I thought I'd drip on the floor, and my nipples were as hard as my clit, both threatening to make me come with the slightest touch.

Too soon, though, Caleb pulled away and put my phone back in my purse. Walking over to the pulley, he lifted me higher and higher still, until my hips hit the ceiling.

"Are you ready?" he asked me once again, making my heart thump, wondering what could possibly be next. We hadn't negotiated anything other than rope suspension, and I worried about what he was planning, knowing needles and canes were being used in the next room.

"I asked, are you ready?" he said, yanking on the rope underneath me and sending me spinning. When I gave him the affirmative answer he was looking for, he reached up to my belly and steadied me.

With great ceremony, he untucked the end of a rope that was hidden beneath the coils wrapped around my torso. Catching my eye in the mirror, he smirked and then pulled on that end of the rope, sending me twirling, whirling and spinning toward the floor. My heart rushed as the hard, black bottom of the room came racing toward me and stopped when I did, only inches away from contact. I cried out, tears rolling from my eyes, aching all over from the red burns that were now covering my body.

Caleb laughed, tying my leverage rope to a post on the wall and reaching back into my purse for my camera. I didn't care who was watching, I didn't care what I looked like in the photos Caleb took; I just wanted to lie there, helpless, crying.

Caleb took a few photos and then put my phone back away, coming over and sitting cross-legged by me, my body hanging lifeless except for the heaving of my stomach as sobs released from somewhere deep within me, somewhere instinctually guttural. He rubbed my head tenderly and wiped my nose with a gray kerchief from his back pocket until my body stopped heaving and my breathing became steady once again.

Putting his handkerchief back in his pocket, Caleb walked over to the pulley and lifted me once again, this time waist high. Coming back over to me, he pulled my rope cage from left to right, sending my body swaying around the room. The rope stung, but I enjoyed the sensation. Caleb pulled me up and kissed me, pushed me away, and then spanked me on the ass as I came swinging back toward him. Back and forth we moved like this for what felt like hours, but surely must have been only minutes. I was wet again, dripping wet, and all I could think about was what kind of rope he had coiled in his pants.

"Please fuck me," I babbled, unable to control myself.

"What was that?" he said, smacking my ass harder.

"Please," I said, mustering up all of my courage, "fuck me. Sir."

He jerked me toward him, lifting me up until we were face-to-face. "You think you deserve that? You think you've been a good girl?"

"No, Sir," I said, choosing my words wisely, knowing my pleasure depended on his whims, "I think you deserve it."

Caleb chuckled. "Good answer," he said, unbuttoning his jeans and pulling a condom out of his back pocket.

*Oh please, yes,* I thought, my mouth watering. I hungered to taste him.

My eyes were level with his zipper and I watched as Caleb exposed a dark black leather harness and gloriously large cock tucked into it. I wondered how he walked with that much hardness between his legs, but my thoughts were stopped as he came toward me and I opened my mouth excitedly. I was determined to take all of him, in whatever way he wanted me, for however long he wanted me. I was his to have.

He was gentle at first, letting me slowly suck, adjusting to his girth, adapting to giving a blow job without having my hands accessible, something that was surprisingly difficult. Luckily, Caleb had patience and helped guide himself into me. Soon, we had a rhythm and I took him deep into my throat over and over again.

In one smooth motion, before I even noticed what he was doing, Caleb pulled out, spun me around and placed his hands on the sides of my ass. It was only then that I realized I had been tied with my ass lifted and legs spread and hoisted to the height of his cock; it was only then that I realized he had planned for everything.

Caleb entered me with his gloved fingers first, slipping easily through my wetness deep into me, spanking my ass with his other hand. I squirmed as he fingered me for a bit, adding more digits as he went, pushing the rope into my clit with his thumb. I let out a pouting cry when he exited me, making him laugh.

"You want something?" he said, running the head of his cock lightly up and around my lips.

"Yes, please," I moaned, pushing back against him, desperate to have him inside me.

"Yes please, what?" he said, moving away from me.

"Yes, please fuck me, Sir," I begged. And with that, he entered me.

Caleb's cock felt amazing, like it had been built to fit my body, filling me with perfect pleasure, hitting every place within me that longed to be touched. He grabbed the ropes suspending my ass in the air and pulled them toward him, over and over and over again, going deeper within me each time. A length of rope rubbed against my clit as he fucked me, and I wondered if he'd put it there on purpose. *Of course he did*, I thought, *he did all of this on purpose.*

From the beginning, Caleb knew exactly what he was doing to me.

My mind went numb as pleasure filled my body, rhythmically building to release. My whole being throbbed as the ropes bore into me with each yank toward Caleb's body, his meeting mine repeatedly until every part of me was begging me to completely let go. "I'm going to come," I sobbed loudly.

"No you aren't," Caleb said, spanking my ass as he thrust harder into me.

"Please, Sir," I pleaded, my body pulling against itself, tensing in the ropes, about to come whether I liked it or not, whether Caleb liked it or not. "Please, Sir, I have to come."

"Not," Caleb said, pushing hard into me, "yet."

I willed my body to cooperate, to wait until I had the permission it needed, but it wasn't listening to me. I was about to burst.

"Now!" Caleb said, and with his one last hard thrust into me we both exploded. Caleb bent over onto me, spent, the ropes holding both of us. "Damn," he said, reaching under me to caress my hard nipples.

"Mmm," I moaned, unable to think complete thoughts. We floated there in silence for many moments, our bodies pressed together, sticky and warm. Eventually, Caleb pulled out, took off the condom, tucked his dick back in his pants and twirled me around to face him.

"Are you ready?" he asked, for a fourth time, bending down to meet me.

Looking into his tender eyes, I replied, "Yes."

Getting up, Caleb released my body to the ground and began unbinding me, one loop at a time, his hands working more gently than before, caressing my bruised, broken being back to life.

When all the rope was off my body, I began to shake, and Caleb led me from the mirrored room to a large, comfortable love seat on the edge of the main dungeon. Wrapping a blanket around me, he held my body as it acclimated to the world outside of bondage, the feelings of longing and release competing within me. I felt so comfortable there, enveloped in his arms, nestling into his protection.

"What's your name tonight, darling?" Caleb asked, brushing some hair from my face.

"Tabitha," I said, curling into his warmth. "Tabitha the cat."

"Well, Tabitha the cat," he said, allowing my body to melt into his, "you were a very well-behaved kitty tonight."

"Thank you, Sir," I purred, my lips meeting his. We kissed deeply, passionately, connected to each other on a visceral level, every synapse of mine on fire with his touch.

And in that moment, I was blissfully, wholly and completely happy.

# LEO RISING

## Suleikha Snyder

The hotel lobby is quiet. Discreet. All palm fronds and polished marble. The men at the desk don't even look up as you head straight back to the elevator banks. Do they know? Do they care? Do they see this kind of thing all the time? The questions excite you and prickle your skin with nerves in turns.

The elevator doors swallow you up into a gilded cage, the walls so clean, so gleaming, that you can see yourself reflected. A little windswept, a little disheveled, your lips slicked with gloss and your eyes bright with need. You look like someone half-done, not quite awake. But that will all change soon enough.

You watch the numbers on the strip light up as the floors fly by. Thirteen. Of course it's thirteen. Because you make your own luck.

The hallway is dark, narrow, accented by the occasional standing vase filled with flowers, but the beige patterned carpet is lush enough to sink with each step you take. It must be a bitch to clean. But that's not a thought you need to concern yourself with. Not here. Not now.

Two turns, one right and one left, and you're at your desti-
nation. The key is suddenly slippery in your hand, but you fit
it into the slot and when the indicator turns green, your breath
expels in a whoosh. The tension of the day goes with it. The day,
the week, the month, the year.

As he knew it would.

He's kind of a gorgeously prescient man that way.

When the door swings open, it's to reveal a modest-size,
tastefully expensive room. And him. Waiting.

He's sprawled across the king-size bed, careless only on the
surface. Because everything he does is deliberate. He staged this
just for you: pristine white sheets wrapped around his narrow
hips, just below the sharp cuts of bone that point like arrows to
his hidden erection. Because he *is* hard. As hard as you are soft.

All he's wearing is the watch you got him for your last anni-
versary, his ring and the smile he's given you every day for the
past six years.

You wouldn't have it any other way. You wouldn't have *him*
any other way.

His dark eyes go half-lidded with knowing, with need, as
you walk all the way into the hotel room and kick off your
shoes. "Surprised?" he murmurs, the word muffled by how he
rests his cheek against his arm.

"Always," you say.

He's not relaxed. Not really. He's…leashed. Waiting. Hiding
his inner thigh because he knows you want to press your mouth
to it. Shielding his cock because he knows you want to get your
hands on it. Teasing you because he knows how much you like it.

The keycard was in an envelope on your desk when you
got to work, a room number and a time scribbled on the front
in his unruly hand. You don't know how it got there, and it
doesn't really matter. Messenger. Courier pigeon. Owl. A late-
night break-in. You can picture him writing, hunched over a

pad of paper, his long hair falling into his eyes. Just the thought
of the bare patch of skin between the edge of his sleeve and
the base of his palm is mesmerizing. There are bits and pieces
of him that, by themselves, could fascinate you for hours. The
whole package is almost too much. But it's all yours. Naked and
golden and dusted with fine dark hair.

You want to sink your teeth into the firm flesh of his shoulder.
Bite his thigh and nibble on the curve of his asscheek. *Not yet.*
So you focus on the teeth of your zipper instead. Buttons. Laces.
You strip for him as he watches you, still with that sheen of
sensual abandon, of languor. Like he's already been fucked into
glorious submission.

Laughable, considering he'll turn on you the moment you're
in his arms. He's your *sher*, your lion. It's all the pretense of
repose and then the leap. He'll go for the jugular, tearing inco-
herent moans and pleas from your throat.

"Rough day?" He tugs at the sheet, turns just enough for it
to slip down over the rise of his cock and the wiry thatch of hair
that nestles it. He's never been shy about his body. You've never
been shy in your appreciation of it. You're certainly not going to
feign the vapors now.

"It's getting better all the time," you laugh, finally closing
the space between you. A little swing in your step and sway to
your hip. A devil in your grin.

He reaches out and catches your fingers, pulling you the
last few steps. The friction of the thick silver ring on his thumb
against the side of your hand is almost enough to make you
come.

The anticipation alone has had you on the edge of orgasm
all day. You wanted to escape the morning staff meeting, lock
yourself in a bathroom stall and touch yourself. You wanted to
call him at noon just to hear him whisper in unprintable Hindi.
But you didn't. You held out.

Because this is better. Going to him. Skimming across the mattress on your knees. Until they meet his chest. Until his lips find the ticklish spot under your left arm. His mustache drags along your skin, his beard stubble rides the goose bumps in its wake. But you don't giggle. No, you just gasp and lean in to his open mouth and his wet tongue, his hello kiss in the strangest, sweetest of places.

And then you push him down, straddling his hips, finally divesting him of the stark white bedsheet. A model without a shoot. That's what he is. Art without an artist. And a lover with only minimal patience. "Tease," you whisper.

He folds his arms behind his head, stretching out beneath you like a vast array of warm sand. "*Nahin.* I am no tease." His voice is a wave hitting the shore, all gorgeous ebbs and flows of consonants and vowels. "Teases don't follow through."

He always does. A key on your desk. A filthy voice mail. Two simple words in a text message. A caress, a tap, a squeeze. They're all promises he keeps. Like to love, to honor and to cherish. And sometimes—only sometimes—to obey.

You reward him, and yourself, with everything you've wanted to do since you walked in the door. A lick of his flat, hard belly. A nip at his shoulder...just sharp enough to make him buck upward between your thighs. And then you take hold of him, hot and throbbing and ready, and you stroke until all his playing at calm turns wild. Until *he* turns wild. Your *sher*, your lion...your man-turned-beast.

"Surprised?" you ask against his lips.

"Always," he gasps into your mouth.

Everything he does is deliberate.

Everything you do together is effortless.

Loving each other like this is at the top of the list.

# ORCAS

## Regina Kammer

Y ou need a vacation." My secretary eyed me with stern sympathy.

"Is it that obvious?" I knew full well my slumped shoulders and the bags under my eyes were telltale indicators. The firm had finally finished the behemoth of a class action lawsuit known affectionately as The Grim Reamer.

"I'll book you something." Her eye roll was punctuated by an exasperated sigh. "Where do you want to go? How about an island?"

"Okay, but nothing tropical." Truth be told, I'm not a beach-and-crystal-clear-blue-water type. Plus, I hate waxing my business.

She shook her head, clearly thinking four years of intense litigation had made me insane. "All right. An island. But not tropical."

And that's how I ended up on a ferryboat skimming past evergreen-covered islets miles from any metropolitan center on my way to Orcas Island, a place so far north my cell carrier sent me a *Welcome to Canada!* text. Definitely not tropical.

But definitely a wonderful place for a vacation, especially in July. The weather was gorgeous, not a cloud in the sky despite Washington's reputation. The ferry was teeming with all types of travelers—retired couples, young families, sporty singles. As a non-outdoorsy, unmarried, almost middle-aged, rest-and-relaxation seeker with a tote bag full of *Cosmo*s and romance novels courtesy of my secretary, I wondered where I fit in.

I was chuckling at that very thought when I realized *he* was looking at me. And when I looked back at him, I'm sure I blushed. He smiled, raised an eyebrow, then went back to reading his book.

He was sitting across from me so I got a glimpse of the cover. *Cycle the San Juan Islands*, with a photo of happy bicyclists in full-on cycling regalia much like what he was wearing. My eyes followed the spine of the book down over his thighs, his knees, his calves.

*Holy crap.* The guy was one solid muscle.

I'm used to dating other lawyers who like to think of themselves as athletic. They *do* ski, and mountain bike, and play tennis and go to the gym, but really only with the intent of letting off steam and keeping in shape until they get married and start having kids and too many beers. Until then, they have nicely honed bodies; I've been known to accept a second date with several of them just so I could get a peek at what was underneath the slim-fit button-downs and flat-front chinos. I've never been disappointed. With the sex, yes, but not with the bodies.

I'd never slept with a hardcore cyclist though.

As I stared at his thick hands holding the book, my eyes were drawn up along his arms, over his biceps bulging against his skintight cycling jersey, all the while trying very hard to make it seem like I was not looking at him. But I must have been too obvious. He stared at me with his green-gold eyes as he threw the book aside with a toss of his coffee-brown hair. Thirty seconds later, he was on top of me, his hungry mouth tasting mine, his hands roving frantically, pulling up my shirt, my skirt, tearing at my panties, then fucking me like a prisoner during a conjugal visit—

Okay, well, that last part didn't actually happen. He sat there and read his book while I averted my eyes and stared at the passing scenery, too embarrassed to pull out my own frivolous reading material. I really needed this vacation.

Orcas Island was quite lovely with its fields of grasses leading to dense forests, its driftwood-strewn coastline, its strange mix of alpaca and deer. I had to admit I was already beginning to feel relaxed.

My friend with the awesome body, now officially dubbed Bike Guy, had given me the most disarming smile just before the ferry docked. I secretly hoped to see him riding along the smooth island roads, his thighs pumping at the pedals. But what would I do then? Stop and give him a blow job? No. I'd probably just drive right on by in my sporty rental.

The B&B was just as cute as my secretary had promised. Two deer looked up at me from the vast lawn fronting the two-story Victorian, then resumed eating when I posed no threat. The proprietor, Charles, and his wife, Madeline, an ebullient couple who were probably much older than they looked, offered me a glass of prosecco before giving me the grand tour.

"The sign-in sheet for the hot tub is on the entryway table," enthused Charles, his zest for the activity overly apparent. "The jets are on a timer. We just ask that you close the cover when you get out and be as quiet as possible after nine o'clock at night."

"The hot tub?" My secretary had failed to inform me of this. "But I didn't bring a bathing suit."

Charles chuckled. "We don't use them ourselves," he confided conspiratorially. "You'll find a robe on the bathroom door."

Later that night, as I walked to the hot tub in the plushest robe ever, with a glass of pinot gris and a trashy romance, I realized my secretary had purposely not told me about it. I definitely would have felt obliged to pack a swimsuit.

And when I stepped into the steamy, churning water, I thanked her. It was far more relaxing in the buff, especially with the pulsing warmth aimed at my lower back.

But I had caught the tail end of the timed jets and they turned off after a few seconds. Feeling uncharacteristically free in my nude state, I decided to explore my little space, trying out all the nooks and crannies of the plastic seats, looking forward to foot jets, neck jets, shoulder jets. When I found the best spot, I relaxed into it, realizing instantly the experience would be so much better with some wine. So I reached across the tub for my glass.

And then the jets turned on.

Right between my legs.

I was startled at first, but a seemingly long-forgotten tingling sensation compelled me to stay in my somewhat obscene position, my butt sticking up as I bent over the strong blast of water. I reached down and pulled back the tender skin covering my clit, feeling the sensual massage more directly. *Oh. My. God.* It was fabulous.

But how long would the jet stay on? Long enough for me to come? Why on earth was I worrying about that? This was better than my vibrator! Better than porn! Better than watching porn while using my vibrator! *Shit.* I needed two jets, one for my cunt...

Praying the timer would not click off, I positioned myself over the gushing spurt, letting it fuck me as I bobbed up and down. My muscles flexed instinctively, welcoming the torrent of water inside. But my clit yearned for attention, and my own masturbatory efforts were not enough. I repositioned so that the jet could focus all its energy on my most sensitive spot, yet somehow I needed even more. Maybe it would be stronger if I got closer...

I spread my legs over the rushing water, angling my hips just so, straddling the full force. Once again, I pulled back my flesh, exposing myself to an intense, rhythmic, pulsing deluge. I closed my eyes, concentrating, willing my body to relax, letting the familiar warmth spread across my belly to hitch in my heart, looping down to tingle my toes, rebounding, striving for the pinnacle, reaching, reaching—

My orgasm exploded, jolting me back as the jet continued its assault on my overly sensitive but very satisfied clit. I had to stifle a little yelp of joy. No need to wake up the whole house.

And then the jets stopped. Funny how they were precisely timed for my sorely needed gratification. I downed my wine, then lay back in a molded seat and let out a long sigh of relief.

At breakfast the next morning, convinced everyone knew about my late-night escapade, embarrassment overtook me. I flushed as I glanced around, expecting to find sniggering and rebukes. Yet the older couple by the window and the family of four in the center of the morning room all seemed oblivious to the fact that they had a shameless floozy in their midst.

One table was empty, the flowery porcelain plate with the crumbs of a delicious orange scone the only clue that a well-fed patron had just left. I soon discovered that the scone was the last course in what turned out to be a breakfast extravaganza, fortifying me to such an extent that I decided to go on a hike.

This pleased Charles and Madeline tremendously, so an hour later I was laden with maps, a water bottle, a sweatshirt ("It gets chilly on the forest paths, dear,") and a great deal of encouragement. Guilt about what I had done in their hot tub flashed in my mind for a split second. They were too nice to me.

I drove halfway up Mount Constitution to the waterfall hike trailhead. It was a moderate trek, one mile down, one mile back, with lovely views and not a soul in sight. Despite the clear and sunny weather, it was, as Madeline had said, a bit chilly under the forest canopy. Still energetic from my breakfast and needing a bit more sunshine, I drove to the top of the mountain.

There was far more human activity at the top. A Civilian Conservation Corps tower, picnic tables, gift shop and toilets attracted those used to even less physical exertion than I. Plus the views from the peak—the highest point in the San Juan Islands according to the signboard—were spectacular. When I turned around to go check out the tower, who should I see but Bike Guy standing at the picnic table stretching out one lean, buffed leg, his Lycra shorts clinging to his perfect ass. Another spectacular sight.

He was talking to a fellow cyclist, an older man, and from their hand gestures and excited chatter, I supposed they were swapping stories about riding up mountains. He glanced my way and nodded with a jerk of his chin as I walked by, a quite unexpected acknowledgment that sparked a blaze of prickling heat that suffused my skin. I went up the tower to the observation platform where I could indulge my private, anonymous view of him. He stretched his thighs as some other cyclists approached, friends of the older guy. They all exchanged pleasantries and swapped a few more stories, then the older guy and his pals said their goodbyes and left the object of my fantasies very much alone.

I looked around. I, too, was very much alone. Until I heard the hard slapping of metal cleats on the stone stairs and saw *him* burst onto the landing, panting, desperate.

"I thought they would never leave."

"What? Who?" I was thrilled and panicked all at once.

"That old man and his buddies. The moment I saw you, I

knew I had to have you." He strode forward, hunger in his eyes.

"Have me?" *Jesus,* I was so wet.

His hands were all over my body, as his mouth descended upon mine. He rubbed the bulge in his tight shorts between my legs before cinching them down just enough to pull out his rampant cock.

"Suck me," he demanded.

I dropped to my knees and drew him into my mouth, tasting his sweat, musky and acrid. He moaned and rocked his hips gently. But I couldn't get enough of him. I grabbed his taut buttcheeks and rammed his cock down my throat. Which was precisely what he wanted.

"Oh, god, yes!"

My nails dug into the thin fabric of his shorts as I sucked eagerly. He came in my mouth with an appreciative groan. I savored every last drop—

The screaming of children in the tower stairs shocked me back to reality.

Bike Guy was still down below, now sitting on the picnic table, and I was still up on the overlook, both of us quite decent.

Oh well.

I smiled pleasantly at the screaming kids as I passed them on the stairs. When I got to the ground, Bike Guy waved at me and patted a space on the table next to him.

I was thrilled and panicked all at once. This time for real.

"You're staying at the Blue Whale Inn, aren't you?" he asked, as I tried to sit as normally yet provocatively as possible.

"Yes," I responded calmly until I suddenly realized he probably knew what I had done the night before. I'm pretty sure I blushed again.

And when I got the courage to actually look at him, his wry smile suggested he knew something very naughty about me.

*Oh god.*

"I love coming here." He vigorously rubbed the tops of his thighs, something any athlete would do, but with him it was terrifically erotic. "Orcas has some good cycling, and Charles and Madeline run a great place." His fingers curved under his legs to prod and massage his hamstrings.

"Hearty breakfast." *Shit. That sounded stupid.*

"Yeah," he agreed with a chuckle. His hands kneaded his hip muscles, his thumbs directed inward, pointing to his crotch. Was that padding? "Have you discovered the hot tub?"

I almost fainted. "Um, yeah." This line of discussion was not going in a direction I wanted.

"I think I'm going to need a dip later." I wasn't sure if he was teasing me.

"So, did you ride all the way up the mountain?" I asked, trying to change the subject.

"Yeah." His manipulations now focused on his inner thighs, tempting me, daring me to watch. "Some of the trails are closed this time of year, which means bikes have to use the road. I'm still recovering from an injury, so that was probably best."

"Oh?" I turned to look at him. He was astoundingly handsome, boyish and chiseled all at once. Even the sweaty brown curls framing his face were charming.

He grabbed his right foot and extended his leg upward. "Less jarring."

I nodded and tried not to stare at his fully exposed crotch. What I did manage to catch a gander of assured me it was not all padding.

"What have you got planned for today?" He put his leg down, then did the same with the other, giving me a view of his butt.

"I plan to find a sunny piece of shoreline and read a book."

"Sounds relaxing." He jumped off the table and flapped his thick, muscular arms a bit. "Well, I'm off. Going down will be a blast." He gave my thigh a little swat. "See ya around."

I watched him ride off, his touch still burning through my jeans and finding its way between my legs to torment me there.

Reading my tawdry romance on a secluded shore was indeed very relaxing. It was frustrating too, but frustrating in a tingly, exciting way. Implausibly, the hero of *Lord Crawley's Craving* had gold-green eyes and dark-brown hair along with the standard rippling muscles—my Bike Guy in a book, except with a stiff collar and riding a stallion. Despite the lack of fellow tourists in my stretch of rocky beach, I kept looking up, abashed, afraid that someone could sense my private infatuation, would know I was wet—drippingly so. Frustration mounted as I could not possibly masturbate in public, even with the dearth of people. My hand ached from restraint. I would definitely need a hot tub experience that night.

Back at the inn, I breathed a sigh of relief upon seeing that no one had signed up for the hot tub. I put my name down for the final time slot. Lord Crawley and I would have a delightful romp just before bedtime.

Once again, I arrived at the tail end of the jets. Fine by me. It gave me a chance to settle in, sip some wine and read to the next sex scene. Lord Crawley was rather impassioned for Maria, his widowed neighbor who was rediscovering the pleasures of the flesh. Those two went at it like bunnies.

*"Maria, my love,"* he growled, *"you inflame me, my body is as the fires of Hades in your presence. Touch me, my pet…"*

The jets came on. I maneuvered myself over one in particular.

*…her fingers curled around his rampant member, feeling the scorching heat…*

I reached down to better expose myself to the pulsing water.

*"Ah, yes, there, Maria. Touch me there…"*

"Hey."

The sound of the vaguely familiar voice sent me lurching back against the side of the tub, splashing water onto the surrounding decking.

It was Bike Guy, standing before me in all his glory. He was magnificent. I think I gasped.

"Can I join you?" He had the most beguiling expression on his face.

"Y-yes." *Oh my god, yes.*

His balls swung seductively as he stepped into the water. He reached for my book, glanced at it with a grunt and a grin, then placed it next to my now-empty glass of wine.

The next thing I knew his mouth was covering mine in the most delicious, succulent kiss, his tongue silky and insistent. His strong arms pulled me against his lean body, his rock-hard erection nudged between my thighs.

"Let's make the most of the jets, shall we?" he murmured as he urged me back into my previous position.

Somehow the pulsing water felt so much better this time around, arousing me quickly, more fully, more wantonly. Bike Guy was behind me, touching me, his body never losing contact with mine.

His fingers dallied briefly inside me before his cock prodded my cunt. God, I wanted him, but I wasn't prepared. I stiffened.

"Don't worry," he soothed, brandishing a condom wrapper in front of me before flicking it next to my book. "I got this covered."

He pushed forward, sliding easily through my wetness, my body welcoming his intrusion, squeezing every inch of his hot, hard prick. I climaxed instantly.

He groaned his approval and slammed inside me, reaching around to expose my clit more fully to the throbbing jets.

I climaxed again, the force propelling my body forward. I clung to the edge of the tub for purchase.

"Relax." It was a gentle command, but a command nonetheless. "I have you."

One beautifully sculpted arm snaked around my waist to hold me steady against the double assault of the pounding water and his driving cock. Counter to my nature, I let go utterly, let him take control, let my body have what it wanted. He was wonderfully thick, filling me, rousing every erogenous zone the jets could not reach, his labored breaths matching the rhythm of his relentless thrusts.

My orgasm was absolutely spectacular. And loud. His hand slapped over my mouth to silence me. He hammered away resolutely until he came with a jolt and a clipped groan. Spent, he bent over me, panting, kissing my back.

The jets turned off.

He chuckled. "Good timing, huh?" He pulled out, and then sat on the edge of the tub to slip the condom off his still-hard prick.

"Fuck, that was fantastic," I blurted. I had to say something after such an encounter.

"Yeah, it was." He smiled and chucked my chin. "Well, I'll leave you to your book," he said with a sigh as he got up and put his robe on. "I got an early start tomorrow."

I just stood in the water, still stunned by the whole thing, and watched him walk away.


I was half-excited, half-embarrassed to go in to breakfast the next morning. How did one handle this sort of thing? Should I move my place setting to his table in a bold gesture of overt intimacy? Did I mutter "good morning," then pretend nothing had happened? Should I follow his lead?

Turned out I didn't have to do anything. As I left my room I just happened to spy him in the driveway, checking a small trailer hitched to his bike. Then he got on and rode away.

I let out a long exhale, of regret or relief I wasn't really sure. I suddenly felt a need to wallow in reliving every second of my very real fantasy. Luckily, thanks to my secretary, I was booked into a spa that afternoon. A massage or salt rub or whatever would be a soothing remedy.

As I poured my coffee I laughed to myself. *Bike Guy*. I never even got his name.

# MORNING'S COME

## Sommer Marsden

It was my birthday and he said, anything I wanted. Anything. I. Wanted.

I'd whispered my fantasy in Riley's ear for years. We've pretended and acted it out in the privacy of our own home a thousand times. And yet, we'd never actually done it.

When he was laid off from his normal job and started working at Fix It Depot, I knew I had a shot. I sat on that information for almost a year, wishing he'd bring it up. But he never did. He talked about working in the kitchen and bath section, described new items, new displays, but never ever did he bring up my fantasy.

I get off on fucking in public. In really weird places. He gets off on teasing me to the point of insanity.

Every time he brought up his assigned department, my face would flush, my pussy would grow wet and I'd chew my lower lip trying to entice—hell, trying to goad—him into suggesting we act out my fantasy.

He never bit. He'd just watch me like some science experiment. Watch my pupils dilate and my fingers war with one another in my lap, a fidgety thing I do with my hands when I get worked up.

Finally, the day before yesterday he asked me. "So, Meg, what do you want to do for your birthday?" He was grilling a steak when he said it and clearly wasn't expecting my answer.

"To fuck in the new shower display at your store."

He paused, stared at me and then grinned. "So, you're finally going to ask?"

"Well, you never offered," I said. I heard the tiny bit of petulance in my voice and hated it. But at least it was honest.

He came at me and I felt the leap of blood in my veins, the tingle of arousal low down in my belly. "That would ruin the fun of watching you ask." He kissed me, dragging his finger from my collarbone down to my belly button. Then a bit lower. He slid his hand up under my sundress, cupped my ass and squeezed.

"What are the best hours?" I asked. The thrill was almost getting caught, not actually getting caught and Riley getting fired.

"To titillate you? To satisfy your dirty-dirty needs?" Riley dragged his fingers up my ass, along the small of my back, coaxing a shiver out of me.

"Yes," I laughed. "Those things."

"We're open six to ten..." He trailed off and rolled his eyes up to stare at the sky, thinking. Then: "I'd say about six thirty. Believe it or not we get a rush right when we open. Contractors, mostly. It lasts about fifteen minutes and then poof! Everyone's gone until about seven fifteen."

I chewed my lip but stopped when he pushed my lower lip down with his thumb. He kissed me, waiting for me to answer. I was having a hard time, considering his hand had run along the elastic of my panties and his fingers had inched their way down the front. The warmth of his skin swept back and forth over my mound. If he would simply push his hand down a bit farther. Part my outer lips, find my clit, touch me...

I sighed and whispered, "Whatever time you say is best. I trust you."

He chuckled, backing me up against the wooden fence as the steak hissed and sizzled on the grill. We might have overdone meat but I didn't care. He pushed down my panties, and finally touched me where I wanted him most. Riley slowly fucked me, curling his fingers against my G-spot until I was trembling, holding on to his shoulders and coming with a nearly silent exhalation.

He kissed my forehead. "Maybe the neighbors saw," he chuckled. Then we went inside and ate. The morning couldn't arrive fast enough.

My fingers were shaking and it was making tying my shoes damn near impossible.

"Morning's come," Riley said softly in my ear. "And soon so will Meg."

I blushed. The heat in my cheeks made me feel lightheaded.

"What if we get caught?"

He shrugged. "We've never gotten caught before, but if we do…"

I waited, watching him as he laced up his work boots.

"Then I find a new job," he laughed.

I smiled. I'd feel awful if that happened, but this fantasy was a craving, a craving that seemed to go right down to the core of my bones. "I'm excited."

He kissed the top of my head. "Me, too. Happy birthday, baby."

The drive to work took forever.

"Good news is, we're short staffed today," he whispered, leading me down the wide cold aisles of the store. Overhead, no-nonsense steel shelves towered, holding everything from plumbing pipes to bug spray to lightbulbs. The store was big and impersonal and perfect.

In his section, there wasn't a person to be found. But every so often, from the maze of aisles, came a random customer. And that was what got my blood flowing fast.

"The one I was telling you about is right...here." Riley pulled me around the corner and we stopped together, right there, in front of a spectacular gray-speckled marble shower display. The doors were open but when he pushed them shut they were thick, textured glass.

My mouth popped open in surprise and awe. I loved it. Riley laughed, and pushed my mouth shut. "You'll draw flies." Then he stepped inside and pulled the doors shut. I could see him... but not. He was a figure there behind the textured safety glass. Clearly a person but not clearly identifiable, not even by gender.

He pushed the door open and winked at me. "Coming?" Then he laughed at his own joke and said, "Well not yet. But soon. However"—he put a hand out to me—"that will only happen if you join me."

"Are there cameras?" I asked, reaching for his hand. My shaking had turned to a more significant tremor as adrenaline flooded my system. My nipples peaked, stiff and tender inside my bra. My panties grew damp from arousal that had built from the moment I awoke. I was having trouble drawing a deep breath.

He tugged me into the shower stall and pushed me to the smooth, cold wall. "Yes. There are. But they aren't at an angle where they'll pick this up. Not even us entering the display." Riley popped the button on my jeans, drew down the zipper. "Speaking of entering. I'd like to enter you very soon, birthday girl. Slide into that wet, slick cunt of yours."

I hummed softly, so turned on I was reduced to noises and not words. I pushed my hand down into his jeans and wrapped my fingers around his cock. I started a slow, easy stroke until he said, more than a little breathless, "Take it out."

We warred with each other and our clothes until I found

myself laughing. But then Riley pushed his fingers inside me and started to thrust and all the laughter died on my lips. I arched my hips, with my jeans pooled around my legs, and met every single stroke of his fingers.

"Hurry," I said, my pussy slick and swollen from wanting him.

Riley was there too—at that sweet spot where desire met need. Turned on, scared, worked up. He nodded and said nothing. I noticed he hadn't shaved and pulled him down for a kiss. The kiss turned fierce, his stubble scratching my face until it burned. He had his jeans down, his cock out and his hands on my hips, pinning me to the wall.

Voices drifted from far off, licking at my ears, amplifying my pleasure.

"—Anyone working in this section?"

And an answering voice: "Guess not."

I bit my lip to keep from laughing. "Turn around," Riley growled. "Put your pretty hands up on that wall while I fuck you."

A shiver marched up my spine, and I obeyed him. Putting my hand with my wedding rings on top of my other hand, I braced myself as I pushed my ass back toward him, teasing him. Tempting him to enter me.

His fingers breached me again, one fingertip finding my clit. He kept me there, heart pounding, suspended in pleasure just a heartbeat away from coming.

I hiked my top up and pushed my upper body to the cool marble for a moment as he ran the tip of his cock along my drenched slit. His other hand came around to the front to stroke and tease my clitoris.

"Hello?" someone called outside the shower stall.

"Hurry," I gasped, my cunt pounding in time with my heart. This wouldn't take long. Not long at all.

People were circling his department. It was only a matter of time before someone found us. Or saw us through the pebbled glass. The realization forced a wave of breathtaking excitement through me.

"Hurry," I said again as he circled my ass with his cockhead. "Stop teasing me. Fuck me. Fuck me," I hissed.

Riley tsked at me but I could tell he was smiling. "The birthday girl is so demanding," he said. But then he was entering me, my pussy stretching to accommodate his girth. I shivered again, and when he touched my clit with a warm fingertip, I came.

"That was easy," he said, kissing the back of my neck.

I could tell he wanted to banter but was a little breathless himself. He was in me now. Fucking me at work. Fucking me in the shower display at work. A shower display—a dream of mine for ages. But it had never worked out. Not until now. Thank god for Fix It Depot.

I pushed back to take him, relishing the possessive feel of his hands on my hips as he got into the rhythm and began to fuck me in earnest.

"I want you to come again," he said, leaning over to kiss the back of my neck. "Come for me, little girl," he said, a little darkness in his voice.

I gasped for air, realizing that his words coupled with my fantasy come true had put in me the position to do exactly that. To come again.

I moaned but quickly cut off the sound when I heard how bad it echoed in the hollow space.

Riley grunted, his fingers gripping my hips tight. Tight enough that I might have a few bruises. Fuck, I hoped so, because the thought of it had me turned inside out.

"Come," he rasped. "Hurry, Meg—" There was warning in his voice.

Outside, the voice called again, "Hello?"

"Jesus, Meg, Jesus fucking Christ—"

He jerked roughly against me and I was right there with him, coming hard enough that I began to moan again without thinking. Riley smacked a hand over my mouth, cutting off my sound, sealing off my air for a second. Just long enough to amplify the swell of pleasure deep inside me.

The voice was closer, calling, "I thought I heard someone..."

We were a flurry of movement. Getting tangled in our clothes, laughing nervously. Fumbling in the small, dark enclosure. I saw the shadow of a person on the opposite side of the glass and almost yelped but Riley caught me by the front of my shirt and pulled me in for a kiss.

"I love you, you crazy woman. Happy birthday." Another kiss, frantic but wonderful.

"Hello?" The voice said again, and damn if she didn't knock on the glass.

Riley cocked an eyebrow at me but pushed the door open and smiled at her. I stepped past him, flustered and amused and so, so happy I felt drunk with it. "I'll take that one," I said, stepping past the woman.

"Why don't we work out the details later today?" Riley said in his best salesman voice.

"Yes, yes," I stammered. "You help this lady and I'll go over things with my husband tonight."

He smiled at me. "You do that."

Then I walked away. When I looked back over my shoulder, Riley was watching me. He winked. I'd see him later and we'd celebrate my birthday. We'd celebrate in several different ways. One of them would definitely involve reliving our morning fuck.

# BABES

## Elizabeth Black

Alex Craig looked at the women sitting with her in the waiting room. A few of them spoke. One came from as far away as California. Alex hoped she had an edge over the out-of-towners because she was a Boston native. Did any of them suspect she wore a jelly rubber butterfly beneath her staid business suit? The tiny sex toy nestled against her pussy, its silent vibrations arousing her so much her nipples hardened against the lace fabric of her bra. *I'm going to walk into that interview horny as hell. It's only fitting, considering what kind of company this is.*

Men who were obviously employees walked back and forth, up and down the hallway, and each one of them looked so scrumptious she wanted to devour a few for an early lunch. It figured such attractive men would work for *Babes*, a company that made elite, expensive sex dolls.

One of the men approached the office where the interviews were being held. He took one look at Alex and stopped dead in his tracks. She nearly gasped at the sight of him. A bright smile creased the sexiest bedroom eyes she had ever seen. The gorgeous man stared at her as if he couldn't quite believe what he saw. *Has he guessed I'm masturbating in a room full of unsuspecting women?* She assumed that man was one of the interviewers, and he noticed her above all the others.

And boy, did she notice him, too! His face was chiseled perfection, most likely acquired under a knife. Broad shoulders filled out his tailored Italian suit. Piercing almond-shaped brown eyes topped with angular black eyebrows stared hard at her face, her breasts, her legs, and her skirt where her pussy was—where that butterfly worked its magic on her. Thick black hair covered his head, and his skin was the color of mocha. *He has some Japanese in him somewhere.* His voice was like honey running over her skin, warm and sticky. She wanted to lick him off, slowly.

"Miss, are you here for the interview?" he asked.

"Yes, I am."

"Good luck." He opened the door to the office at the end of the waiting area and walked inside.

Alex looked around the room. The women fidgeted, nearly as nervous as she was. She badly wanted this job. When she'd received an email from Elena Carter saying she wanted to meet her, she'd danced around her apartment. She had grown tired of her current job months ago. Now, here she sat in the *Babes* waiting room surrounded by beautiful women, getting off with a sex toy. The butterfly's vibrations worked her clit until it swelled, demanding attention. She squirmed in her seat, each shift of her delicious bottom driving intense jolts of pleasure into her hot pussy. Brushing a hand through her hair, she moaned. Several heads turned in her direction, and she fought the urge to break out in laughter over her cheeky little game.

More than anything she wanted to come and come hard, but she needed to concentrate on why she'd come here in the first place. She had a job to win!

After she finished filling out the application, she signed and dated it. That application asked unusual questions such as would she cut her hair, what foods did she like, and did she enjoy using sex toys. As her butterfly buzzed away she mouthed a resounding "Yes!" *Be daring, girl.* She noted in her application she was wearing a clit stimulator and it felt *sooo good.*

A tall redhead walked out of *Babes*'s main corporate office. The woman's face was a mask; it was hard to read her expression. Alex didn't know from looking at her how her interview had gone. She could tell the woman was a model, since models were good at mastering the aloof look.

A classy woman in a tailored black suit stood in the open doorway. Her face was ashen with shock as she stared at Alex.

"You. Come in here. Now." Her deep voice resounded around the room, making heads turn.

Alex wondered what she had done wrong. Everyone stared at her with both envy and mirth as she very self-consciously crossed the room. For a moment, she feared the women could hear her butterfly humming, but the toy was so silent there was really no danger of that happening. She felt clumsy, tottering about in her stiletto fuck-me pumps carrying her oversized portfolio.

The woman closed the door behind her when Alex entered the office. Two men, one of them Rod Tyler, whom Alex had recognized from photographs on the company's webpage, stared at her openmouthed.

"I told you. Isn't the resemblance incredible?" the gorgeous Asian man who had spoken to her in the lobby said, giving her the once-over for a second time, making her feel ravished with his eyes alone.

"Oh, my holy sweet Jesus..." Rod Tyler said in a soft, low voice.

Alex froze, feeling the intense gazes from all around her.

The only part of her body that moved was her eyes—and her butterfly. Those intense vibrations and standing in full view of their scrutiny aroused her like never before. Her gaze flitted from the man who spoke with such honeyed warmth, to Tyler, and to the woman. Tyler's eyes, on the other hand, were on the move, gazing from her hair to her face to her breasts, waist, hips and legs. He stared pointedly at her breasts. She resisted the urge to button her jacket. She was used to being given the full-body once-over by men, but getting it in such a blunt fashion during a job interview was a little unsettling—yet alluring. *This is the most unusual job interview I've ever had. I wonder how much more enticing it will get?*

"Please don't be alarmed, Miss..." Tyler said.

"Craig. Alexandra Craig. Please call me Alex."

"We're being rude. Alex, please have a seat." He swept one arm toward a leather chair in front of his desk. Alex sat down. "I'm Rod Tyler, owner, president, and CEO of *Babes*. Elena Carter and Jackson Beale are my VPs. Please pardon the way the three of us are gaping at you openmouthed."

"Isn't the resemblance uncanny?" Elena Carter whispered. She stood a few paces behind Alex, next to Jackson Beale. Alex could see neither of them but she felt their professional scrutiny on every curve of her body. She hoped the back of her suit wasn't too badly rumpled from squirming in that uncomfortable chair in the waiting room.

"Yes, indeed, the resemblance is blowing my mind. It's like seeing Danielle in the flesh, live and speaking to me."

"Danielle?" Alex asked. By now she was completely confused but curious as to whom this mysterious Danielle could be.

"Danielle is our latest top-of-the-line model. She hasn't even been released yet," Jackson's disembodied voice sang from behind her. "Have you ever modeled for us?"

"No...yes. Well, you had a call about a year ago for head and body shots for use on your dolls. I sent you a few and promptly forgot about them."

"That must be it then," Tyler said. "It's so strange seeing you here after working on Danielle for so long. Also…" He glanced at her application, and raised his eyebrows. "Under the sex toys question you wrote *You should see which one I brought with me. It's one of my favorites. And it feels sooo good!* Are you saying what I think you're saying?"

Alex crossed her legs and tilted her head to one side in a coy position. "It does. I'm wearing a butterfly. It's my favorite toy."

Jackson shifted from behind her. "You're wearing a sex toy? Right now?" The arousal in his fevered voice made her nipples so hard she swallowed to control herself.

She felt the heat of a blush rise on her cheeks. "Yes, I am. And it's turned on. A strap-on, battery-operated butterfly." Her butterfly's silicone wings hummed against her pussy lips as the toy's body hummed against her clit. She shifted in her seat, excited from both the effects of the toy and the thrill of the interview. Knowing she was getting off excited her as much as watching the astonished and pleased looks on their faces. Deep down, Alex enjoyed a touch of exhibitionism.

"And does it feel *sooo* good?" Jackson mimicked her tone in her application.

"You bet it does!" The four of them laughed when Alex's ecstatic exclamation echoed around the room.

"I like you more and more every minute," Tyler said.

"So do I," Jackson said. "What do you think? Is she the one?"

"I like her very much," Elena said.

"She sold me on her talent to begin with, but the sex toy was a nice and unexpected touch," Jackson said.

He continued to speak from behind her, out of eyesight. Not seeing him made their conversation even more thrilling since she had to imagine the bald expressions of lust and interest on his handsome face. "I agree. She has proven she enjoys decadence as much as we do. You can count me in."

"In that case, Elena, would you be so kind as to fetch Danielle?" Tyler said. "I'm sure Alex would like to meet her. Alex, the job is yours if you want it."

"I...but you haven't...it's mine? I don't understand."

Tyler laughed. It was a friendly laugh but the sound of it left Alex with a disturbing feeling that she was the unsuspecting victim of a delicious prank.

"Really, Alex, it's quite all right. I already reviewed your resume when you mailed it earlier this month, before you set up your interview. Your credentials are impeccable." She heard the door open behind her. Tyler reached into his desk and brought out an employment contract. He held the contract out to her, along with a fancy stone-encrusted pen. She took both. "The job is yours. Please read the contract and sign at the bottom. Don't forget the date. But first, there's someone I'd like you to meet. Turn around."

She did, and was shocked to see her doppelganger sitting in a chair behind her.

"Alex, meet Danielle."

The latest, not-yet-released, top-of-the-line *Babes* model could have been her changeling, left by playful sprites in her crib twenty-four years ago when her mother wasn't looking. She was dressed in an expensive pin-striped business suit. The mini-skirt barely reached Danielle's butt. *My butt; she has my ass.* Danielle's hair was the same auburn shade as her own but it was cut in a long pageboy. Alex's corkscrew hair fell to her elbows.

"Oh my." Alex couldn't think of anything less ridiculous to say.

Jackson laughed. "I can only imagine how you must feel. It's like finding your long-lost twin, isn't it?"

"Worse. It's like finding an android that's going to replace me. I watch too many bad science fiction movies."

"Good taste in movies, food, and sex toys," Tyler said. "We're going to get on just fine."

"May I touch it...her?" Alex asked.

"Absolutely. Tell me what you think of her skin," Jackson said.

Alex walked to the doll and ran her hand down one arm. She wondered how much she should touch. Taking a chance, she reached beneath the doll's blouse and squeezed one huge breast. *My breast, although hers is bigger and nicer than mine.* Her face warmed as she blushed, and she smiled at how she must look inspecting her own double.

"Her skin feels very pliant and soft. I can squeeze her arm and the flesh gives. I like that. Her breasts also feel soft and realistic. They're very squeezable."

"We improved on her breasts for the newer models. I'm glad you like her."

She stared at the hem of the skirt that nearly touched the doll's crotch. *How forward may I be?* She had the job, but she was wary of making too personal a statement about her doppelganger. Alex swallowed hard, and decided to be blunt. A jar of condoms sat on Tyler's desk. What else was that desk used for? Could she make it clear to Jackson that she wanted him?

"How is she to fuck?" Alex's throat felt dry as she asked the question. She looked at Jackson. She wanted to hear his answer more than anyone else's. As she stared at him, she slipped one hand beneath the doll's miniskirt and slid two fingers into its pussy. The material molded tightly about her, pressing her fingers together. She didn't detect any vibrators inside, nor did she suspect the pussy was removable.

Her legs shook with excitement from both handling the doll

and the vibrations that assaulted her pussy from that butterfly. She took a deep breath and looked Jackson squarely in the eye. Did she arouse him, in the flesh and in the form of a doll?

Wanting some distance between herself and the doll, she retreated to her seat. "I'm very tight, and I throb when I come. Have you thought of putting a bullet vibrator in the doll's pussy? Or make it a removable, vibrating pocket pussy? I've used ben wa balls to strengthen my pelvic floor. My lovers liked that very much."

"Lovers?" Jackson straightened up in his chair. Good. She had his attention. "How many lovers do you have?"

"I had four, but I broke off the relationships. They were very clingy. I don't like to be tied down." *I can't believe I just said that...*

"You don't?" It was no wonder Jackson curled up one lip at her. His eyes danced and gleamed in the fluorescent lights. *My god, he is easy on the eyes. I wonder what he must think of me with the way he's teasing me and twisting my words.*

"Not in that way. I've never been tied down to a bed, if that's what you mean. I might like it." Feeling warm, she pressed her legs together. The butterfly buzzed against her throbbing pussy, and she threatened to burst into an orgasmic puddle of goo any second now. Badly wanting to remove her jacket but resisting the urge, she wondered if such sexually charged discussions were commonplace at *Babes*. She wasn't sure how she felt about it, but the sex talk shouldn't have been a surprise since this was a sex doll company, after all.

The lighthearted sexual banter sure beat the boring business-as-usual atmosphere of her current employer.

She recrossed her legs as her skin overheated, partly due to the temperature in the office and partly due to the fire in her groin. Sweat beaded on her chest. That butterfly would make her come in an instant if she didn't compose herself.

"We've never had a complaint about our dolls from the men who've used them," Jackson said. "I like your points, though. Rod, could we insert a computer chip to make Danielle and the others vibrate when you push a button?"

"I'm sure we could. We'll look to research and development for that. It's a wonderful idea. That and the removable pocket pussy. Thanks to Alex."

The sexual charge in the air felt palpable and overpowering. The three of them held her gaze for a few beats too long, showing intense interest. They eyed up her long, slender legs and her full breasts without even a hint of propriety. Her heart raced at the obvious sexual attention, and she felt herself grow more at ease. *I'm going to like working here...*

"How's that vibrator holding up?" Jackson asked with a voice full of arousal.

"I'm about to burst," she said with a self-conscious laugh. *I can't believe I'm doing this and talking so openly about it to a man I just met, but these people and this company bring out my inner sex kitten.* "I sometimes wear my butterfly to work. It helps pass the time."

"I'm sure it does," Tyler said.

"What kind of butterfly is it?" Jackson asked, staring into her eyes with so much passion she wondered if he wanted to take her right there in the office. There was that bowl of condoms, after all. "Is it a plain one or does it have a built-in dildo?"

"This is my plain one. The dildo one is at home."

"You mean you have a *second* butterfly?" The astonishment in his voice amused her.

"I have four. This one is my favorite. It has the biggest wingspan so it stimulates my clit and labia in the best way." She locked her gaze with his, not even allowing herself to blink so she wouldn't lose his attention. "I review sex toys so I have an entire closet full of them. That's why I applied for work here.

I have lots of experience with sex toys, both cheap and very expensive."

"You sound out of breath."

"I am." Although her attention was riveted to his face, she was keenly aware of the other two in the room who eyed her up with as much scrutiny.

"You're aroused?"

"Yes. And I'm almost ready." She swallowed hard as the saliva in her mouth dried up. She wanted a glass of wine more than anything—except a roiling orgasm.

"You're not the only one who's aroused. May I hold your hand?" His intention was clear. He wanted to come with her, in full view of the top people in the company. His exhibitionist characteristics intrigued her, and brought out her own wish to expose herself, something she rarely dared to explore. She'd let her fear outweigh her fantasy of showing off the most wanton side of herself. What was happening to her? She'd never before been so risqué, but this interview and these people emboldened her. She wondered if Elena and Rod were voyeurs. They seemed to get off on the sexual repartee.

Jackson held out his hand and she took it. His palm felt cool to the touch. She was sure hers sweated like a stallion that had been ridden too hard. He rubbed his thumb against her palm in a gesture so obvious she was surprised she wasn't shocked. Was the atmosphere at *Babes* always so sexually charged? She hoped so.

His breathing became very labored while the other two stood by silently and watched without touching themselves. Such a curious situation to be in, but she enjoyed it so much she wanted more. She stroked Jackson's hand with her fingers, gently scratching the back of it with her nails. They continued to stare into each other's eyes. She leaned forward in the chair so the butterfly had direct contact with her clit, and the instant peak of arousal startled her so much she squeezed his hand.

He smiled at her before taking her hand in both of his. He then guided her other hand to his groin. The moment she touched his erection she gasped, ecstasy overpowering reason. He was large, thick with passion, and he wanted her. She ground her pussy into her butterfly as she rode the waves of orgasm, and he pressed her hand hard against his cock as he groaned, overwhelmed with his own climax.

She didn't stop him when he wrapped his arms around her, body jerking, heart pounding in her ear. She gripped him tightly until their passions subsided, and then they separated, tidying up their clothes. Rather than cowering in shame, Alex felt rejuvenated and eager for more excitement. She looked at Jackson and smiled. He gave her a wicked grin.

A sigh from her right brought her back down to earth. Tyler stretched in his seat and Elena leaned against the wall, smoking a cigarette. The pleasant scent of clove filled the room. They enjoyed the silence for several glorious moments.

"I see we're going to get on very well," Jackson said, his voice mellow in their shared afterglow. "When can you begin?"

"Begin what?" She raised her eyebrows.

"Begin *working*," he laughed.

"I need to give two weeks notice." Her crooked smile enhanced her playful mood.

"That works," Tyler said.

"Consider it done. If you don't mind, would you come in this weekend for orientation? Saturday starting at 10:00 a.m.?"

"I'd be happy to. And thank you for hiring me."

"Then it's settled." She pressed a button on her phone and spoke to her assistant. "Andrea, please tell the other women thank you, but we have filled the position."

"I'm very happy you hired me." Alex monitored her tone so she wouldn't sound as if she was gushing. "I've wanted to work for *Babes* for a very long time. Thank you for hiring me."

"No, thank *you*." Jackson said. "If you hadn't modeled for us we wouldn't have noticed you so quickly." His eyes creased at the corners as he smiled. "Of course, *I* would have noticed you immediately."

*He's too good to be true.* Alex shook hands with the three of them. Their handshakes were as firm and as confident as their manner.

Jackson walked over to her and with a slight hand to her elbow he escorted her to the door. "Also, when you dress for Saturday, wear your sexiest suit and underwear. We at *Babes* like to look good from the inside out. Not that you'd have a problem with that."

She knew her time with *Babes* would be the time of her life.

# ENTRE NOUS

Darsie Hemingway

She was waiting for me in the bathroom. That was the plan all along. She would wait for me in the bathroom, I would excuse myself from the table and we would fuck like maniacs in the end stall, perfectly silently, me standing on the toilet so that only one set of feet showed, then we'd exit one at a time. I'd go back to the table. Mitch would go back to her car and drive home. It seemed like the best solution to having to endure dinner at a stuffy French restaurant with my parents.

Of course she had to gag me. There's no other way I could possibly remember to be quiet. At first I used to make noises even with the gag, moaning and whimpering, but eventually, with some practice, I got accustomed to it, to the thickness of it stuffed inside my mouth, its weight against my tongue, reminding me to be silent. Eventually, I could come like a freight train and make not so much as a peep.

It was the noises, I realized, that were taking the intensity out of my pleasure. They were, like a slow leak of air from a tiny hole, a way of draining my breath, leaving less energy to go to my pussy where I needed it. I think it was my body's defense mechanism—my pleasure center was afraid of exploding if it really felt anything and everything it could.

It wasn't until Mitch fucked me in the back stacks of the library one day that it dawned on me to stop being such a loud-mouth. Oh, it wasn't just being in the library. I was good at shifting my moaning and screaming to a form of heavy panting in her ear. But even that was funneling my energy outside of my deepest places. It was while she had me pressed up against the stacks of books, my legs straddled, fingers gripping the cool metal ledge of the shelf, getting pounded from behind by Mitch's fist, that my eyes lolled back into focus for one moment, just long enough to land on the spine of a book. *The Power of Silence*. It was an omen dropped like a fishing line into the musty, murky library basement, and its words jostled in my mind, long after our library adventure.

Silence. It gave me something to think about. Not the kind of silence from holding your breath—that can put your power on pause. No, the kind of silence that builds power is what I craved. The kind of silence that comes from breathing not from your mouth, but from deep in your body. That silence. The kind of silent breath that drops like an anvil into your pussy on a deep inhale and shoots like a firework up your spine when you exhale. The kind of silence that allows things in the air to mani-fest as physical form. Silence that engraves itself into an ecstatic scribbling deep within you. An etching your body traces over and over again, and remembers as bliss. Silence that makes me rake my fingers down Mitch's back until she bleeds a holy trail of pleasure/pain.

So there we are in the bathroom.

I'm standing on the rim of the toilet. My hands are pressed flat to the cold metal of the stall. My eyes are locked on Mitch's eyes, while her fingers slip in and out of my creamy, tingling pussy ever so slowly. She's only giving me a teaser. I know she's packing. *More,* I mouth, silently. She smiles and shakes her head slowly. She starts to rub my clit with her thumb while her fingers keep slowly fucking me. I am getting so hot and I want more, more, more, so I can explode in sparkling luxury and practice my perfected silent peak. Mitch just smiles at me with her brilliant blue eyes. She slows down. I give her an exaggerated pouty face and pull my dress down low to show her the spill of my boobs over the lacy edge of my French black bra. I know she can't resist that.

She falters and licks her lips. I start to pinch my nipple and roll it between my fingers. I let my mouth drop open into the shape of silent longing, and arch my back. Mitch shakes her head no and reaches into her pocket for the gag. Its black leather strap clinches the bulbous black ball that will soon be snug in my mouth. She buckles it around my head. It's a heavy hand holding my tongue. It calms me. It brings me back to my center. Mitch's hand picks up speed.

I keep my feet solid against the toilet and continue to press my palms against the walls, while I start to writhe my hips, just ever so slightly, toward Mitch's hand. Shifting to meet her like this, in the most subtle way, always takes me to the next level. While I rock my pelvis slightly back and forth, Mitch's long fingers snake their way deeper into my pussy. I can feel the arch of her finger roaming the canal of my pussy for that soft spongy spot that makes me come like a waterfall. Her thumb is rocking against my clit, making it hot and shiny.

Mitch hikes my dress up with one hand and bunches it to the side, grabbing hold of my hip bone and the dress so she can see me better. She wants to watch my hips fucking her hand and I know it. She wants to smell the ripe spicy scent of my pussy as it gushes. She wants to see my black lace panties stretched taut between the trunks of my thighs. She wants to keep my dress clean because she's thoughtful like that. Mitch widens her fingers inside me and fucks me deeper and I start to lose it. *No sounds, no sounds,* I tell myself. The gag is an anchor in my mouth. A stone that holds me here. An anvil tied to my tongue. I can feel the pleasure, deeper, broader, longer. I can feel my body opening like layers of inaudible bubbles popping, like a thousand roses blooming, every muscle busting into a quiver. I'm opening, opening, opening. My insides get slick, wide and starting to spill. Come rushes out of me like an avalanche. I can feel my pussy convulsing around Mitch's fingers, the shock waves loosening my core to a column of ripples. She doesn't stop.

Mitch keeps fucking me with her hand: deliberate, slow, intentional. I can feel her desire pushing its way into me. She pulls my dress up higher and starts kissing my belly. It feels so good. Mitch. Her tongue teasing the rim of my belly button, her breath like a warm chain of kisses along my waist. She licks the edges of my hip bones and nuzzles my belly button. And while she kisses me her hand just keeps fucking me. I want to tell her to stop, that I have to go back to dinner, that my parents are surely wondering what's taking me so long, that…but I can't do it, it feels too good. I couldn't anyway, with the gag in my mouth, and the promise of silence between us. I can't say a word.

She knows I need to go back to dinner. The agreement was for the quickest, quietest fuck in bathroom history. Beyond these walls there is a bustling restaurant full of luscious plates of food arriving to tables with tidy, elegant place settings, a vase of flowers, wineglasses, rich creamy desserts. Mitch notices my attention wavering at the same time as her internal clock goes off. Mitch is wired liked that. She pulls her hand mostly out of my pussy, just leaves two fingers hooked inside on the edge of my pubic bone. She looks at me with her sparkling blue eyes and smiles the most loving, sweet grin. She gently removes her fingers, giving my pussy a little pat as they leave, as if to say, *See you later.* Her dimples flash as she removes the gag. I stand there, still tingling, as her hands knowingly remake me, guiding my breasts back into their lacy cups, pulling my panties up so tenderly, smoothing my dress down and combing my hair back into place with her fingers, still fragrant with the aroma of my pussy. She kisses me longingly on the mouth and slips out of the bathroom stall. I imagine her sneaking out the back door of the restaurant, getting into her truck and driving home. I'll see her later.

I wait a moment, then hop down from the toilet, wash my hands and notice my face in the mirror, brightly alive and slightly flushed. I leave the bathroom, headed back to the table with a bigger appetite and a mind ready to compose a night of surprises later for Mitch.

# DOLLYMOP

## Malin James

The last thing Faye needed was a corset. Corsets were for women with abundant breasts and gorgeous thighs. Faye did not have these things. What Faye had was bone. She was tall, thin and delicate. A former lover had once remarked that he could count her ribs through her skin. She did not have curves. She hardly had breasts. She almost never wore a bra.

This did not stop her from wanting a corset though. She saved a portion of her paycheck every month without acknowledging, even to herself, what she was saving it for. Before long, she had over a thousand dollars and a file full of images, each one a snapshot of her greatest wish—to be sexy, not fragile. To be dangerous and strong.

She was dithering downtown on her lunch break one day when she wandered down a side street and stopped short upon seeing something she'd never seen before:

FLEUR DE LYS CUSTOM CORSETRY

Faye stared up at the oval sign. It was glossy black wood with ivory letters, whose borders shone with glints of dull gold. It looked like a sign that had traveled through time, been restored, and then carefully hung back up. She took a step forward—close, but not too close—to the open shop door.

She was fortunate enough to live in a city where corsets and piercings and tattoos were at a premium, but she had never seen a boutique like this. It was smallish, with large, leaded-glass windows, as if the original panes still hung in the casings. Three dressmaker's dummies stood in the window amid a swath of ivory silk. All three wore corsets in distinctive designs. *No, not corsets*, Faye thought, drinking in the watered silk, tailored poplin, and romantic black lace. They were more than corsets. They were the most beautiful things she had ever seen.

Suddenly, another figure joined the three in the window. Faye startled so hard that she dropped her bag.

"Oh god, I'm sorry," a woman said, coming through the door and into the quiet street. "I didn't mean to scare you, I just wanted to say hi. You looked like you were enjoying the window."

Faye stared at the woman. She was small and buxom, with a mass of glossy black hair that tumbled artfully down her back. And she was wearing a corset too—a smart, sexy, businesslike thing in gray pinstripes. It looked killer with her tailored, menswear suit.

"Uh, you okay?"

The woman was regarding her now with a mixture of concern and compassion, as if she were looking at a kitten in a box, which is exactly what Faye felt like. Nervous, Faye cleared her throat.

"Yeah," she said, staring at the woman. Her eyes were a bright, uncanny green. Eyes shouldn't be that green. "Yes, I'm okay..."

The woman's face relaxed. "Good, honey, I was—"

"How long have you been here?" Faye turned bright red. She never interrupted. She rarely ever talked.

"About a month," the woman said, not seeming to mind. "We've been around for ages but this is a new location."

Faye nodded, feeling awkward. The woman stuck out her hand.

"I'm Cat, by the way."

*Of course you are*, Faye thought, looking into the woman's bright, feline eyes.

*Tyger, Tyger, burning bright...*

"I'm Faye," she said, managing not to embarrass herself again.

"Nice to meet you Faye. Do you want to come in?"

"Oh, no, I couldn't. I mean...I'm not really built for corsets."

Cat tilted her head, visibly assessing Faye's measurements.

"Actually, Faye, you're built great for corsets. You just need the right one."

Faye looked at her, unconvinced.

"Tell you what. Why don't you come in? You don't have to buy—you can just look around. You might be surprised."

Before Faye could decline, Cat gave her a friendly wave and ducked back inside. Still mulling uncomfortably, Faye's feet took the initiative and carried her through the door.

The inside of the shop was as elegant as the window display—honey-blonde wood, antique white walls and fabrics draped artfully over almost ever surface. And scattered carefully throughout the room, more seamstress's dummies wore more corsets, some as lingerie, some as outerwear and some as the bodices of gowns. There was even a wedding dress. Drawn as if by magnetism, Faye went from dummy to dummy, fingers hovering an inch above the fabrics she was too afraid to touch.

"Beautiful, aren't they?"

Faye jumped.

"Oh, sweets, I'm sorry. I scared a year off you—again! I was just going to offer to walk you around."

"No," Faye said, blushing. Suddenly, she felt like an idiot for being there. "It's okay. It looks like you're about to close."

Cat shrugged. "My last fitting just rescheduled. It's really a perfect time."

Faye looked into her sharp, green eyes—sharp, but very kind, she realized. Slowly, Faye relaxed. "Okay, sure."

"So," Cat said, as they meandered around the showroom. "If you could be anything, what would it be?"

"Beautiful," Faye blurted out, before covering her mouth with her hands. Cat stopped walking and looked up at her. Even in her platform boots, Cat was half a head shorter than Faye.

"You know you are, right?"

Faye shook her head, mortified.

"No...that's not what I mean."

Cat looked at her, waiting, giving her space. If this was part of how she sold corsets, Faye thought, she was very good at her job.

"I mean, that I want to *feel* beautiful. I want to feel sexy. Like...like a woman, I mean. I'm not. Look at me. I've got no curves."

To her utter humiliation, Faye felt like she was going to cry. Cat pulled a little square of silk out of her pocket and handed it to her.

"You know, honey, a corset isn't going to do that."

Faye's heart shrank. Seeing the look on her face, Cat went firmly on.

"Let me start again. What I mean is, a corset *can* give you curves—hell, it can do things to your body that will make you fall in love—but it can't *make* you feel beautiful. You've got to do that yourself. Right?"

Faye nodded. "Right. I know."

"But," Cat went on with a cheeky grin, "I've got something that will goddamn help you get there. The Dollymop."

"The Dollymop?"

"The Dollymop. C'mon. Take a look."

Cat led Faye out of the showroom into a small consulting area off to the side. She flipped through a book of patterns and, finding what she wanted, turned the massive thing around to show Faye.

"That, darlin', is the Dollymop Overbust Custom Design."

It looked more like an architectural plan than anything else. Faye cocked her head. She wasn't quite sure what she was looking at. Seeing the difficulty for someone who didn't speak seamstress, Cat got out a book of photographs and set one beside the pattern so Faye could see.

The girl in the photo was skinny—even skinnier than Faye— but the Dollymop corset, rather than making her look like a little girl playing dress-up, accentuated her sleek, lithe build, so that her bony shoulders and prominent collarbones looked sculptural, and—Faye had to admit—flat-out gorgeous above the ivory satin and lace.

"Oh my god," Faye breathed, as a thrill of something like arousal snaked through her. Cat sat back in quiet triumph.

"I know, right? I've got one—they work well on most body types—but Dollymops really shine on women like you."

"Like me?"

"Yeah, you know. Tall and ethereal. You're not a standard type, which means that a standard design won't do you justice—no sweethearts for you. But in the right one? Jeez. Knockout."

"I want one," Faye said quietly. For the first time in her life, she was acting with conviction.

"I'd love to make you one. But I should warn you up front— they're expensive."

Faye met Cat's gaze, level and calm.

"I have over a thousand dollars."

Cat raised a brow and considered her.

"Well, hell," she said, smiling, "depending on fabrics, that will buy you two."

Faye nodded, feeling fuller and surer than she'd ever felt.

"Then let's do two."

Six weeks later, Faye was back at the shop. Cat had taken copious measurements and spent over two hours with her going over customization and requirements. Given that Faye wasn't currently seeing anyone, she had no intention of using the corsets as lingerie, so she opted for fabrics that could be worn with clothes—one, a tailored chocolate wool and the other a dark rose silk with deep gold stripes.

Cat had told her to wear something she would pair with the corsets for the final fitting, so Faye had treated herself to a black pencil skirt, which she wore with her favorite stack-heeled boots.

"Today's the day, my lovely Faye," Cat said as Faye came in. All of a sudden, she came up short. "Wow. There's something different..."

Faye shrugged, surprised that Cat would notice. Faye *felt* different, though she wasn't quite sure how. All she knew was that ever since she'd put the down payment on the Dollymops, she'd had a feeling of heightened self-awareness, as if her body was waking up. And the dreams. Oh god, the dreams. After years of muted desire that she'd tucked away in flannel pajamas, Faye was having dreams that woke her up with wet panties, swollen bits and aching pink nipples. She'd even started touching herself, something she'd never felt comfortable doing before. Of course, she didn't tell Cat any this.

"I'm sleeping well," she replied.

Cat narrowed her eyes. "Well," she said, obviously deciding to let it go, "keep it up. You look good."

"Thanks," Faye replied, tucking a chunk of hair behind her ear.

"Now," Cat went on, getting down to business, "come back for your fitting. I'm dying to see how they look."

Faye followed Cat back into the workroom, where a cheval glass stood beneath a swath of brocade. A small, wrought-iron chair completed the space.

"Go ahead and put your bag on the chair," Cat said, pulling out an invoice. "You can wear both of these under or over your clothes, but for this fitting, I want you to try them on without a shirt. If they fit that way, they'll fit with everything else."

Faye nodded, dropping her bag on the chair and watching as Cat removed two boxes from a fully stacked shelf. The boxes were both glossy black ovals with FLEUR DE LYS coiling along the front, a direct echo of the shop's sign. For the first time, it occurred to Faye how much attention to detail had gone into this place. Her delicate, fine-boned body flushed. That meant that the same attention to detail had very likely gone into the corsets she was about to wear. For some reason, Faye found this notion incredibly arousing, though she didn't know why. Her body had just never felt that important before.

Cat brought the boxes to the worktable and set them side by side. Then she motioned to Faye.

"Open them up, sweetie pie."

Holding her breath, Faye did.

Nestled within the ivory tissue of the first one was the chocolate wool, looking structured and confident and uncompromisingly sexy. Faye's hands drifted over it, stroking the faint, white lines that striped the soft fabric. Then she moved on to the second box.

The tissue in this one was a dull, antique gold. Nestled beneath the folds lay another corset, this one of rose and gold silk. The rose made a dusky background for the dark gold stripes, which were only a shade or two darker than the tissue it rested in. The whole effect was one of sensual confidence. There was no come-on in that box. It was all *come to me.* Faye's hand went up to her lips. Cat looked pleased.

"Here, honey. I'll help you try it on."

Cat lifted the rose and gold Dollymop out of the box while Faye unbuttoned her shirt. The air in the workroom was cold and her tiny nipples tightened into pretty little buds, nearly the same shade as the rose-colored Dollymop. Normally, Faye would have been mortified to be standing there, topless, in front of someone else. But she wasn't. Her attention was entirely on the corset in Cat's hands. Her body was leaning toward it. She ached to try it on.

"Here, let me lace you up so you can see. Later I'll show you how to do it by yourself."

Faye nodded, not trusting herself to speak.

Slowly, Cat worked her way up Faye's narrow back, tightening the laces that pulled the corset more closely to her ribs. All the while, Faye's body softened, molding to fit the structure of the stays.

"There," Cat finally said. "Go ahead and turn around."

Holding her breath, heart pounding, Faye did. The woman in the mirror was tall. Faye blinked. And really fucking *sexy*. She turned to examine the elegant line of her waist.

"Oh my god," she whispered. Cat stepped back and smiled.

"I'll say."

Rather than accentuate Faye's tiny bust, the Dollymop compressed it, so that her clavicles and shoulders were displayed like a sculpture's. The long line of her neck swept into the slope of her shoulders like a perfect, inevitable form, while the corset sleeked her torso and nipped in her narrow waist. Faye twisted again, and grinned.

"Look! I've got an ass!"

Cat laughed. "Yes, my girl. You do."

Faye stared at herself in the mirror, only partially registering Cat's presence. Taking her cue, Cat drew the brocade curtains down around her.

"I'll give you a minute. Let me know when you're ready and we'll try on the other one."

Faye nodded absently, running the length of her body with her hands. With a happy, feline smile, Cat dropped the curtain down.

"Wow," Faye murmured.

The color was high in her cheeks and her pulse beat hard in her ears. Beneath the stiff fabric of the Dollymop, Faye's nipples began to ache. She shifted her spine, enjoying the rasp of the lining against her breasts. Suddenly, she had to touch herself. Casting a look over her shoulder, Faye listened hard for Cat. She heard her out in the showroom, talking to another client, Faye presumed. Good. She'd have just enough time. She hoped.

Bending at the waist, which was easier than she'd expected given the Dollymop's structure, Faye breathlessly lifted up the hem of her skirt and tucked her hand into her panties. The stiff ridge of the corset's bottom edge pushed hard against her hand, urging her fingers down and in, through her softly trimmed curls to her sex. Hand shaking, she stroked one finger over her sensitive vaginal lips. She shuddered, shocked at how very good it felt. Faye looked at the curtain. It was still firmly closed. Then she turned back to the mirror and focused on her reflection.

Cautiously, Faye stroked herself, until her finger slipped into her pussy as if it belonged there. Faye bit her lip. She was so hot and wet that a little gush of juice coated her fingers and hand as she stroked her delicate inner walls. Faye's vision swayed. Hiking up her skirt as high as it would go, she sat down in the little chair and spread her legs, allowing the corset to extend her back and hold her up straight. Nestled just visible between her thighs, her pussy pulsed and ached.

Using her body's moisture for lube, Faye dipped her finger in again before joining it with a second. Her thighs began to quiver and her chest flushed above the Dollymop as she focused on what was happening between her legs. Removing her fingers again, she stroked upward, slowly, trailing her juices along the outer folds of her labia until she found the tiny, swollen knot of her clit at the apex of her sex. Holding her breath, Faye pressed down and began to rub.

Outside of the curtains, Cat conducted business, but inside, Faye was bringing herself closer and closer to her peak. She'd never had an orgasm before—not with herself and not with a man. She somehow knew if she was ever going to be able to feel that, it would be here, in front of the mirror, leaning into her own hand while her body swayed in the Dollymop.

Faye stroked more firmly, more quickly, more confidently as the pleasure in her body built. Her narrow hips rocked and her spine flexed, unexpectedly supported by the Dollymop's structure. Faye leaned forward, enjoying the compression of her torso as she watched herself in the mirror and brought herself closer to the edge.

She was beautiful. She was a woman. She was dangerous and strong. She was special. She was something. She was someone.

Flushed and breathing heavily now, Faye parted her vaginal lips. They were plump and ripe and ready—she couldn't believe how sweet they looked. Suddenly, Faye's body took over and she plunged three fingers into herself while she circled her clit with the fingers of her other hand. The amount of coordination something like that required would have intimidated her weeks before, but now, riding herself, riding her own image, gorgeous and full and powerful in the Dollymop, she brought herself up to the full swell of her first orgasm.

Pleasure swept through Faye. She moaned and her head fell back, but her hand kept going, giving her what she so desperately needed. Wave after wave spilled through her as the mirror and the corset and her own strength kept her back straight, her neck long and her shoulders loose as she rode the climax out.

Finally, the pleasure began to ebb, and Faye tipped her head forward so she could look into her own eyes. They were drowsy and bright. She looked happy and alive. *You are beautiful*, she thought.

Carefully, Faye removed her fingers from deep within her sex and straightened her skirt. She'd just adjusted the line of the Dollymop when Cat came back in.

"Faye, honey, are you okay?"

Faye pulled back the curtain.

"Yeah. I'm more than okay."

She grinned. Cat grinned back.

"Do you want to try on the other one?"

"No, it's all right. It'll be perfect. They're perfect. Besides," Faye said, smiling shyly, "I want to wear this one home."

# BEST LAID PLANS

## Oleander Plume

By nature, I am a voracious planner. Every aspect of my life is thought out beforehand, then written with perfect penmanship inside my daily log. My spice rack is alphabetized, my panties sorted by style and color, even my refrigerator is strategically organized by food groups. I wake at precisely five o'clock every morning to begin a daily routine that never wavers. One cup of coffee that I sip while perusing the newspaper, followed by a shower. The next sixty minutes are spent styling my hair, applying makeup and dressing in the outfit I laid out the night before. Every button is fastened, every detail is scrutinized. It is my life, my way, my choice.

Not everyone agrees with the way I do things, unfortunately, which I suppose is why I was served with divorce papers last year. George and I were married for ten months before he packed up and moved in with his mother, citing "irreconcilable differences" as the cause of our breakup. When I pressed him for more details, this is the conversation that followed:

"Help me understand, George. Perhaps I can change."

George rolled his eyes at me like an impudent child. "Change? You? Is there room in your daily schedule for that?"

"What is that supposed to mean?"

"You schedule everything. Every. Fucking. Thing."

He threw his hands up, which caused the sock he was holding to fly across the room. I hurried after said sock, attached it to its partner, and then placed the pair in the cardboard carton he was filling with his belongings.

"See? This is exactly what I'm talking about. We're in the middle of an important discussion and you go chasing a fucking sock! And don't get me started on your daily routine. At first, I thought your need to organize was sort of cute. But when you scheduled our sex life, well, that was the last straw."

"In my defense, I scheduled five separate slots for sexual activity. I fail to see how you could possibly complain."

He sank onto the bed and sighed. "The sex was great, Doris. Otherwise, I would have left after the first week."

"So, this is it? Our marriage is over?"

"Yes, it's over. Mainly because you drive me up the fucking wall."

"I see." I peered into the carton he was holding. "You've packed that all wrong. Toiletries should be placed in their own container, in case of spills and such."

After I helped him repack all of his moving cartons, I said goodbye to George and married life. Living alone again gave me ample time to reflect on my life in general. I wondered if I was too tightly wound, and fantasized about how my life might change if I could become more spontaneous. Such ideas led to thoughts of sex, and since I wasn't getting any, those thoughts began to drive me crazy. I was bursting with pent-up sexual longing and feared I might implode. After I confided in a female friend, she offered to set me up with a gentleman acquaintance of hers. To make it less awkward, I decided I would host a small dinner party, so that I could get to know the gentleman in question before making my decision to proceed with a proper date. The guest list and menu were carefully chosen, keeping in mind each person's dietary requirements. All that was left to do was purchase a protein selection for the main course. The local meat market was well known for its quality cuts, so I stopped there on my way home from work.

The bell on the front door tinkled merrily as I pushed it open. Immediately, the smell of raw meat permeated my senses as I headed toward the counter. Behind pristine glass was a dazzling display of filet mignon, New York strips, even some lovely prime rib beef roasts. Leaning over the counter was an equally ravishing display of meat. Man meat.

My body tingled from the inside out as my eyes roamed over his bulky frame. He was roughly six foot six, with bulging biceps and a cleft in his strong chin. Wavy dark brown hair spilled over his collar, giving him a bit of a devil-may-care aura, which I have only recently found appealing. The hunk was deeply engrossed in a paperback novel. It was quite a treat to come across a man who was not only devastatingly handsome, but a voracious reader as well.

"Hello?"

He startled a bit, then peered up at me with vibrant blue eyes. "Oh, hello, miss. I didn't even hear the bell."

"John Grisham?"

"No, the name's Mack."

"I meant the author." He flipped the book over and glanced at the cover.

"Right, Grisham. I'm at the exciting part." He set the paperback facedown on the counter so that the pages were splayed open.

"Tsk, tsk. You'll break the spine that way." I dug through my pocketbook and found an old receipt that would serve as a proper bookmark. I tucked it inside his book, and then placed it back on the counter with a flourish. "There. Much better."

"You must really love books," Mack said with a grin.

"Yes, I'm a librarian, so I suppose you could say books are my life. I also write in my spare time, although I don't have much of that."

I made a big show of peering into the glass at the slabs of red flesh, hoping he would notice my ample cleavage. In an attempt to break my routine, I had purposely left a few of the buttons on my cardigan unfastened. The thought of his deep azure eyes roaming over my breasts made my panties dampen.

"I'm hosting a dinner party tomorrow night. For six."

"Did you notice that I have crown roasts on special this week?"

"Yes, I did. They are quite tasty, aren't they? I just adore the little paper frills that cap each bone, as if the dinner itself dressed up for the occasion."

"Always enjoyed that myself, although I'm usually afraid I'll end up eating one by mistake."

He erupted in the most delightful laugh, one that was deep and rich. It was then that I noticed the adorable dimple in his right cheek, and was overcome with the sudden urge to dip my tongue inside of it. Thoughts of seducing him flooded my brain, but did I dare? He was a stranger, albeit a lovely one, so bulky and masculine. I was newly divorced and a bit shell-shocked but aching with sexual needs. The ticklish feeling in my clit spurred me on, and I decided to flirt a bit.

"So much delicious looking meat. This eye of round roast is so plump. Do you think it would be juicy?"

"If you cook it nice and slow, it would be very juicy." The way he drawled the words made my nipples hard.

"Hmm, so many choices. I like the look of these T-bones,

they're so thick, I can almost feel them in my mouth." I licked my lips for emphasis.

"Are you stuck on beef? The reason I ask is that I have some great pork loin over here. If you marinate it for a few hours, it's very succulent."

I ran my fingers over my throat as I perused the selection. The tangy smell of blood mixed in with the musky scent of Mack's aftershave was making me delirious. A trickling sensation distracted me as I grew even wetter between my legs. I wondered if Mack could smell my sex, and the thought made my cheeks blaze crimson.

"I do love pork." I looked up at Mack and smiled. The front of his apron was stained with reddish-brown blotches. His barrel chest pushed against the rough fabric as he leaned over to get a better look at me. "It has a nice mouth feel, almost sensuous."

"You're right, miss, pork also has a very delicate flavor." Mack ran his fingers through his hair, and shifted from foot to foot. I could tell I was getting to him, which excited me even more.

"Indeed. So delicate, it's almost sweet, don't you think?"

"Definitely. These butterflied pork chops are nice. What do you think?" Mack asked as he ran his thick index finger down the splayed center of one pink-fleshed chop. It reminded me of a woman's labia, spread open and dewy, waiting to be massaged by a warm, wet tongue.

"Those do look very tender."

"They're even better if you pound them a little."

Mack teased the fatty edge of the pork chop with his fingertip, and I whimpered slightly as I imagined that same finger teasing my clit as I lay before him, naked and willing. I nervously tucked a lock of red hair behind my ear as I browsed further. A row of fat chicken breasts caught my eye. Since we were teasing each other so well, I couldn't resist remarking on them.

"These breasts are so voluptuous, I suppose the men at my dinner party would quite enjoy them."

"Some guys like large breasts. Me, I'd rather sink my teeth into this nice rump roast over here. See how nice and round it is?" He gave it a pat and I giggled.

"Your sausages look divine. Do you stuff them yourself?" They were plump, and so perfectly phallic, I longed to put one in my mouth, even in its raw state. A trickle of sweat ran down the back of my neck, and my heart began to race.

"Sure do. My grandfather's secret recipe. I use all natural casings. Mine are a little longer and fatter than most, so they fill up the bun real nice," Mack said with a wink.

"They certainly are. I don't think I've ever seen any that were quite this stout. I mean, they're positively swollen. May I get a closer look at one?"

"Sure." Mack pulled a square of wax paper out of a dispenser, then reached into the cooler and wrapped it around one of the links. He handed it to me like it was his own cock. I almost swooned.

"They look even bigger up close."

"I stuff them good." Mack watched in fascination as I squeezed the tube of meat in my fingers, then inhaled the aroma.

"I love the smell of fennel. It's so sensuous." I looked at the piece of beefcake behind the counter and smiled. "It feels so good in my hand, I would love to feel it in my mouth."

"If you like that, I have something in the back room you'll like even better."

"Really? I would be quite interested." I bit the tip of my index finger, then darted my tongue over it. "Quite."

The small gesture was not lost on Mack. He walked around to the front of the counter and took my hand. I almost hesitated. Engaging in impromptu sexual acts with perfect strangers was not in my repertoire, but the longing won out. I dropped the sausage on the floor as we quickly headed to the rear of the shop.

"It's back here, in my office."

Mack's office was a cramped room containing a desk, a chair and a filing cabinet. As soon as the door was locked, I dropped to my knees, lifted Mack's apron and nuzzled his generous bulge. He let out a small groan as I unsnapped his jeans and yanked down the zipper. With both hands I gripped denim and silk together, then tugged. Mack's hard cock made a grand entrance, a sight that made me quiver.

"My, my, this is grade-A prime."

"It's also aged to perfection." Mack chuckled. "What's your name, beautiful?"

"Doris."

"Well, Doris, you aren't like any librarian I've ever met before."

"Darling, I'm going to take that as a compliment."

It is my sincere belief that you can't even begin to know a man until you have been nose deep in his manhood. Oh, how I love to pleasure a beautiful cock with my mouth, and Mack's penis was especially alluring. The silky shaft was the perfect length and width; it stretched above a lightly furred sac that hung heavily between strong thighs. I couldn't wait to taste every glorious inch. First, I lifted that erect cock and sucked one firm testicle into my mouth. My nostrils were filled with the heady aroma of meat juice from Mack's apron mingled with the spicy scent of his scrotum.

"Is that one big enough for you?" Mack's voice was husky with lust, and reverberated down my spine.

"Yes, it certainly is. It's perfect. Thick and meaty, yet tender and succulent." I circled the flared head of Mack's cock, and tasted the delicious saline fluid that dripped copiously. "It's also delectably juicy."

As I sucked the spongy tip, I cupped the balls in my right

hand, and kneaded gently, while my left hand snaked into my moist panties. My clit felt like it was three times its normal size and throbbed exquisitely. I took as much of Mack between my lips as I could, and reveled in the feeling of my mouth being so delightfully full of cock.

"Oh, baby, that's damn good."

"This hunk of meat needs to be savored."

I nibbled on the tip and Mack let out a sexy growl. His fingers curled into my hair as he arched his back in pleasure. I slid my tongue up and down the full length of his shaft, then buried it in the recess that was just under the tip.

"That's really nice."

I loved the fact that I was pleasing him, crouched with my knees pressed against the dirty linoleum like a common tart. I pulled his cock straight down, then licked the place between it and his pubic hair. My nose was buried in the bristly patch and I inhaled. He smelled of shower gel and lust, of raw meat and testosterone. I stood up and looked him in the eye.

"I'm really in need of a nice stuffing."

"First, I need to taste you."

Mack removed his apron, then lifted my skirt while I bent over the desk. He pulled my pink lace panties down to my ankles, and then carefully worked them over my shoes. My moist folds were twitching under his gaze as he spread me open wide. He groaned as his tongue took its first taste.

"Even better than the finest filet."

His tongue flicked over my clit, then worked its way up to my opening. I surrendered completely, giving in to his warm mouth.

"Am I tender enough for you?" I asked, somewhat breathlessly.

"You sure are, baby. And juicy, too. It's dripping down my chin."

His lips returned to my clit and he tugged at it firmly, while

I writhed in pleasure. I lifted my body slightly, and pulled up my cardigan and bra together. I loved the way the cold metal desktop felt against my hard nipples. My ardor grew until I was ready to burst.

"Please," I moaned.

"Not yet."

Mack continued to dazzle me with his amazing oral talents. His tongue traveled from the tip of my clit to the top of my asscrack and every place in between, over and over until I was almost pleading for mercy. When he paused to tease my anal bud with the tip of his finger, that's when I began to really beg.

"Please, I need you inside. Now."

Mack pulled me up until I was leaning with my back against his broad chest. He teased my nipples with his fingers as he kissed my neck.

"Are you sure you're ready?"

"Yes, don't make me wait." My voice sounded thick with desperation, which mirrored what I was feeling. Nothing else in the world mattered except that man's hands and that man's cock. I wanted to be fucked hard and proper. "Now, Mack."

"You've got it, kitten." Mack turned my body around to face him, then lifted me by my hips. I wrapped my bare legs around his waist as he impaled my pussy with his stony cock.

"Yes, yes, fuck me!"

I crossed my ankles behind his back and drove him in deeper. His hands were gripping my ass, and he had no problem holding me up with his muscular arms. Without warning, he leaned in close and captured my lips under his. This anonymous afternoon fuck had turned into something else entirely. Waves of delicious excitement coursed over me as his tongue and his cock invaded my flesh.

Mack leaned me up against the doorway, while he continued to thrust. I gripped his shoulders and felt my body clench as I was brought to the edge of climax. My clit was rubbing against his coarse pubic hair, sending ripples of euphoria racing through my core.

"So tight and hot," Mack murmured.

My pussy tightened around him like a bear trap as I surrendered to orgasmic bliss. Soft mewling sounds floated up from my open mouth as I squeezed him between my thighs. He sped up his rhythm, causing the door to bang loudly on its hinges. Then he slowed down, turning his movement silky as his fingers caressed my ass. One finger slid between my cheeks and teased my puckered hole.

"Would you like...?"

"Yes, I would like. In fact, I demand."

He pulled his cock out of my pussy, then stood me on my feet. My knees threatened to give out, so I quickly bent over the desk once more. Mack gently kneaded my asscheeks while he covered the small of my back in kisses.

"Mack, please, I need you, now!"

His cock was so well lubed from my own juices, it slid inside easily. I could hardly breathe as the tender area was stretched and filled so carefully by Mack's large shaft. He was gentle and slow, taking time to let me adjust before burying himself inside.

"Oh!" I gasped when he began to thrust in short, pleasing strokes. "It's so divine!"

"You're a dream come true, Doris," Mack murmured.

His cock pulsed inside my ass, taking me once again to the pinnacle of climax. He came first, filling my insides with liquid heat. Then I fell over the edge, clamping down upon him as I slammed into a powerful orgasm. I gripped the sides of the desk and hung on for dear life as the tiny aftershocks made my pussy tremble with delight.

Mack rubbed my lower back as he pulled out. I felt his semen drip down, soaking my already wet folds with his sultry essence.

Like a true gentleman, he wiped my bottom with some paper napkins, before pulling me into his arms and covering my face with kisses.

"Where have you been all my life?" he said huskily against my lips.

I couldn't speak. All I could do was cling to him while I tried to catch my breath. We stood there in silence for a few minutes, softly caressing each other as we floated back down to earth. Mack finally broke the spell, and helped me back into my panties, then adjusted my skirt while I pulled down my bra and buttoned my sweater. I carefully tucked his spent cock inside his jeans and zipped his fly. We walked back out into the front of the shop, holding hands and smiling.

"I think I've decided on the crown roast," I said breathlessly.

"Perfect choice." He weighed it, then wrapped it in crisp brown paper and placed it into a grocery sack. "On the house."

I blushed as he handed me the bag. "Thank you, Mack."

"You're welcome, Doris. By the way, I'll have New York strips on special next week."

"I'll be sure to stop by. Very sure."

"And I'll be sure to stop by the library."

I headed for the door, and then stopped. Schedule be damned, spontaneity was my newfound friend. "What are you doing right now?"

Mack's eyes lit up. "I was going to take one of these filets home and grill it up. Maybe make a little salad."

"How about this—you grab two of those, and follow me back to my place. I'll cook while you pour the wine."

"And will you be dessert?"

I grinned, cheeks flushed, heart racing.

"Play your cards right, and I might even be breakfast."

# LIPSTICK

## M. Birds

The first time she sees Jack is like a punch to the chest, left of the breastbone, over the heart. There's a drag show that night, and Hannah is doing neon-pink shots with Naveen and her awful friends—total lesbian studs or whatever, catcalling girls, grabbing at their crotches and acting like shitty men for the most part. Anyway. A few pink shots in—raspberry vodka or something disgusting—Roxy Diva is onstage lip-synching for her life, when this woman walks into the bar who makes Hannah almost fall out of her chair. She looks like she stepped out of a Fritz Lang film—long legs, black coat, dark eyes. Hannah can imagine kissing her at the end of the movie, only to have her throat cut. Hannah bets she smokes, bets she tastes like whiskey, bets she closes her eyes like she's grieving when she comes.

"Put your tongue back in your mouth," Naveen tells her. "Have you never seen a drag queen before?"

*No.* Hannah says it to herself before she says it out loud. "No, she's not, that's—"

"He doesn't perform much anymore, but he used to. Once

I asked him about his lipstick and he tore my head off. Pretty much a total bitch."

Hannah watches the queen's long fingers curve around her glass of red wine, watches her tongue gently lick across the rim. She's too beautiful for this bar, or he is, or whatever; drag queens mix up Hannah's pronouns. The point is, this person stops the shitty pop music, makes the whole glittery vortex coalesce into a single point of gorgeous, angry mystery.

Christ, it's been way too long since Hannah's gotten laid.

That first time she sees Jack, Hannah utters a silent and blasphemous prayer that he is trans and bi at least, but no such luck. Naveen's awful friends quickly chime in; he's a dude who fucks dudes, and Hannah should keep it in her pants. And Hannah does.

She doesn't see the drag queen again for almost two months, even though she starts becoming a regular at the weekend shows. Naveen tells her it's pathetic, and all right—it is. Hannah's had straight friends make the mistake of falling for gay men, and it doesn't ever end well. And hell, Hannah herself has a strict "no straight girls" policy; she may be many things, but she's not a masochist. If she has the odd startling dream about kissing her way down the queen's elegant neck, unfolding those long legs and burying her face between them— well, dreams don't mean anything. Jack has breasts and a cunt in those dreams, anyway; it's so far removed from reality that Hannah can just delete it from her mind (preferably after a hot shower and a bit of alone time).

It's gotten so bad that the next time Hannah sees the drag queen—slinking in out of the rain, enveloped in a huge black coat—she can barely look at her, convinced that the whole sad fantasy is written in bold type across her face. Naveen mocks her ruthlessly: "He's gay. And you're a dyke, in case you've forgotten. You wouldn't even know what to do with him."

That's not necessarily true; Hannah came from a small town where no one was out, least of all her. She fucked boys in high school and even in college, but when she moved to the city and realized women were on the table, that was pretty much all she wrote. Women turn her on in a way men never did, make her all white hot and liquid and boneless. And yeah, she's taken the women's studies classes; sexuality is a spectrum, and she's not against men, or anything...she's just never looked at one and wanted to eat him alive. She's never wanted to suck the burgundy lipstick from one's mouth.

Hannah makes the mistake of looking up then, and realizes with a shock that the drag queen is looking at her from across the bar, masses of shiny men and women writhing between them, but somehow their eyes catch. There's scorn in the queen's gaze, thin upper lip curled like calligraphy, but there's also sadness there too. Hannah tears her eyes away. It feels too intimate to witness.

"We need to get you some pussy," Naveen's friend tells her, and that pretty much takes care of the rest of the evening. In the end, Hannah goes home alone and comes into her hand, thinking of the drag queen's white fingers sliding against her tongue.

It goes on like this. She sees her mystery drag queen rarely, and almost always alone. Hannah has more wild dreams, and the dreams bleed into her waking moments; she can't entirely blame her subconscious anymore. Naveen tells her that she doesn't even know him, that she has built him into some mystery woman in her head because he looks hot and brokenhearted; it's totally superficial and unattractive. Naveen tells her that she might vaguely resemble a scruffy little boy, but it doesn't mean she can trick a gay man into sleeping with her. Naveen tells her all of this, and Hannah knows she's right. It's a crush, that's all it is, and she'll get over it, because that's her only option. She's a lesbian, for Christ's sake.

She is sitting by herself, the night that it finally happens. Naveen and her awful friends have gone to play pool in the other room, and Hannah had a terrible day at her shit retail job, and just wants to drink her beer in silence. Her hair is a mess and her clothes are just something she picked up off the floor, and there is no reason that this is the night, but it is.

She's a few beers in, possibly too many, when someone sets a tumbler of amber liquid in front of her. She looks up to see the tattooed bartender smiling at her. He nods across the bar where the drag queen sits by herself, drinking the usual glass of red.

"No shit," Hannah says, without thinking.

"I know, right?" The bartender winks and turns away.

Hannah smells the drink, and suppresses a recoil. Whiskey. She's had a couple of bad nights with this stuff, doesn't touch it if she can help it. The drag queen is watching her, eyes wide and solemn, and Hannah feels that look against her skin like a razor. She tosses her drink back in one swallow, doesn't even shudder, makes her daddy proud. She puts the glass down on the table and crosses the bar before she can change her mind.

The floor tilts slightly beneath her, but she chooses not to think about it, planning her opening line. *Thanks for the drink*, she'll say. *Great dress*, she'll say. *Fuck me*, she will not say, even if she's thinking it, even if it's rolling through her head like awful lyrics.

"Not much for whiskey, I take it." The drag queen speaks first, and all Hannah's plans are ruined. She had not expected a British accent. Neither had she expected such a low, sweet voice. It makes her mouth water.

"I thought I did okay," she manages, embarrassed, and the drag queen glances up at her through long, dark lashes. "Thanks, I mean."

"By rights you're the one who should be buying me drinks. With the way you're always looking at me."

"Um." Hannah cannot possibly respond to this. Fuck her fucking lack of a poker face. "So, can I buy you a drink?"

"Another time," the drag queen says, taking a sip of wine. "Are you a lesbian or what?"

Hannah almost chokes herself in surprise. When she can speak again, her voice is rough.

"Um, yes?" she says, and then continues, nervously, "that wasn't supposed to be a question, it was a yes. Um. You?"

"Not a lesbian," the drag queen says, wine leaving a stain of red around her upper lip. Hannah finds herself licking her lips, and the drag queen laughs. For a laugh, it is a surprisingly harsh sound, like it could just as easily be a knife. "You get that this is all, like, wrapping paper?"

"Yes," Hannah says. "My friend saw you perform once."

"Must have been ages ago. I don't do it anymore."

"Then why do you—?" Hannah made a vague gesture meant to encompass the heels, the dress, the legs, the legs, the legs.

"I've been told I'm much prettier in lipstick. Certainly did the job where you're concerned."

Hannah wishes she had ordered them drinks; she's far too sober for any of this.

"What songs did you do?"

The drag queen scoffs. "Sad bastard stuff. Cat Power, Marlene Dietrich sometimes. Such a drama queen." She gives Hannah a brief once-over, pressing her thin lips together, before tipping the rest of her wine back.

"Fuck it. Do you want to get out of here?" she asks.

*God yes*, Hannah does not say. *Yes to everything, yes to all of it.*

She wants to, but instead offers, "I don't even know your name," because she's not like this, she doesn't hook up with people whose names she does not know, she goes on dates and buys flowers and—

"Jack," the drag queen says, eyebrows knitting together as if it's a name she doesn't like. He doesn't like. His name is Jack, and he is a dude who fucks dudes, and what the hell is Hannah even doing?

"Yes," Hannah answers, and Jack stands in a gust of perfume, sweeping through the bar without even bothering to see if Hannah will follow. But she does—of course she does. She sees Naveen and her other friends gaping at her from the pool table, Naveen giving her a look somewhere between outrage and disappointment. Hannah shrugs at her.

Outside the bar, it has gotten cold in that violent, prairie way: a sudden smack to the face. Jack is waiting on the sidewalk, lit cigarette held loosely in her lips. His lips. The smoke and his frozen breath mingle in the air, and when he breathes in her direction, Hannah realizes what the inside of his mouth will taste like. She decides she cannot wait to find out, and leans up on her toes, sliding her open mouth across his like some tipsy, lovesick teenager.

"You're mad," Jack says, shaking his head. He leans down again and they kiss properly, wet mouths and tongues, until Hannah is dizzy with it. He tastes like cheap cabernet sauvignon and cigarettes.

"This is mad," Jack says when they pull apart, but he doesn't mean it—or if he does, he means "mad" in the best possible way. Hannah laughs and follows him home.

His apartment is only two blocks away, and they don't speak on the walk there. The only sound is traffic rushing by, and the crunch of their shoes in the snow. Hannah stares at the seams that run up the back of Jack's tights, and wants to follow them with her tongue. They've barely gone through his front door when he crowds her up against it, tongue licking into her mouth. Hannah sucks on it until he moans, bites down until he shoves her back, panting.

"Drinks," Jack says, not a question. Hannah nods, heart pounding in her throat. "I'll be right back. Make yourself at home."

He disappears into the kitchen, and Hannah takes off her heavy coat and hangs it over a chair. She stands for a moment, twining her hands together and desperately overthinking everything, before moving to sit on his couch. Jack returns, some sort of mixed drink in each hand. He's taken his jacket off, and is wearing a short, clingy black dress. It's the least clothing she's ever seen him in, and she can't stop staring at his collarbones. No one should have collarbones like that, it's not fair. She wants to lick them.

"Thought I'd try gin this time," Jack says, handing her a glass before sitting down on the couch beside her.

"Lucky guess," Hannah says. The drink burns prettily down her throat.

"Full disclosure," Jack says softly, "I haven't done this in a while."

"Slept with a woman?" Hannah asks.

"Slept with anyone."

"Kiss me again," Hannah says. Jack takes a long drink before setting his glass down on the coffee table. He leans forward and she leans back against the arm of the sofa. This is real, this is happening. She's had this dream before, but when she lifts her hand to Jack's throat she can feel his pulse leaping, and she isn't asleep. Her fingers tangle in his wavy hair, and she brings their mouths together as if she's done it a thousand times. In her head, she has.

"Christ," Jack murmurs when their lips part, leaning over her again, crushing her into the sofa cushions. Her hands find a courage she's never had before and encircle Jack's waist, toy with the hem of his dress. Out of habit, they travel up his ribs to squeeze one breast, and at that Jack pulls briefly away.

"It's just...not..."

Hannah knows the difference between padding and flesh, and she bites Jack's neck in response.

"Doesn't matter."

In her dreams, she sucked on his full breasts until he screamed and begged her to fuck him. Or her. Or—whatever, this is good too. She can feel him hard against her hip, and it scares her a little. She hasn't given a blow job since sophomore year of college, and it's been longer than that since she let a guy fuck her. But she would let him, she thinks. If he keeps the dress and the lipstick on, he can do whatever he wants.

"Bed," Jack says, mouth trailing up her neck. Stubble rasps against her skin. She'll be all red and rashy tomorrow, but tonight all she cares about is locking their fingers together and letting him drag her into his bedroom.

Oh god, she's in his bedroom.

Jack doesn't turn the light on, but he flinches when she slides her hand up his smooth thigh.

"That's not who you want," he says quietly, disengaging her hands and pulling her on top of him into bed. His fingers slide over her hips to the crotch of her jeans—habit, Hannah guesses—because he freezes briefly when he doesn't find what he's looking for. Fine, then. He wants something else. Hannah can at least give him part of it.

This is where it all goes foggy. Hannah watches herself from a distance. Saying "lube," and finding a bottle in her hand. Jack swearing, on his elbows and knees. Her hands on his hips. Her fingers inside him.

"Fuck, oh fuck," Jack gasping, back arched, all soft and submissive and honey-sweet.

In the dark, Hannah thinks, this could be a woman in bed with her. This pale, gorgeous creature could be a woman, and Hannah could be knuckles deep in cunt, and then it would make sense why she feels like coming without even a hand on her.

Jack's dress pushed high on his back, Hannah's lips on his spine. Reaching between his legs without thinking, hungry for wetness and skin. Jack pushing her hand away.

"That's not who you want."

He's helping keep the fantasy alive, and Hannah should be grateful. She should be. She uses her free hand to unbutton her own jeans, slide her fingers past her underwear. She's so wet it's almost embarrassing, and she rolls her clitoris between two fingers, grinding against her hand. Jack pushes his hips back and forward, fucking himself on her fingers, jerking himself off, and Hannah's going to come any minute, she can feel it in her ribs and the arches of her feet, bearing down on her like light, like morning, it's coming, it's coming…

"You are so fucking beautiful," she gasps. Jack jerks his hips, faster, faster, wet slap of his hand on his cock, sharp as music.

"Fuck me, fuck me," he hisses, and Hannah does.

She doesn't know what time it is when she wakes up the next morning, only that there is a man in the bed and he is watching her. She flinches, before remembering where she is. Jesus Christ, how did she fall asleep? She can vaguely remember taking her clothes off and—yes, she's naked, they're both naked, and she's in his bed. It's beyond mortifying, and she's about to apologize when she meets Jack's eyes and then, she can say nothing. Nothing at all. He must have taken off his makeup while she was sleeping, and his hair is short, tucked behind his ears. He looks older without eyeliner, creases on his face no longer covered by concealer. In the early morning light, his eyes are such a pale gray that she almost can't bear to look at them. They are the color of winter funerals. She raises her hand to the juncture of his neck and jaw, his pulse fluttering like a bird.

His thin lips are pressed together tightly, and they twitch when she touches him.

"Good morning," he says quietly, placing his hand on her pulse point as well, mirror images of each other.

"Good morning."

She slides her leg over his because it feels natural, and when it brings their bodies closer together she feels his cock, hard and wet against her leg. He gasps at the contact, and she takes him in her hand, without thinking, because this is who she wants. He does not move for a moment, staring into her eyes like she has done something shocking and unforgivable. Then his hand is on her thigh, sliding higher, higher, before one finger slips inside her. He adds another when he feels how slick she is, and Hannah almost wails with gratitude. It's so good, it's perfect, and his mouth opens, tongue a dark wine-red as it traces his lower lip. Hannah wants to kiss him so much it makes her stomach ache.

But she does not.

He presses his forehead against hers, and she strokes him in time with his fingers twisting inside her. How long has it been since she had a cock in her hand, not a rubber one but a real one, with a pale, gasping man attached to it? She slides her hand up his shaft, running her thumb through the precome at the tip of his cock, before licking her thumb, tasting heat and salt and morning. Jack abruptly rolls away, and Hannah has a brief moment of panic, because they are sober now, and there are really no excuses. It's not last night, and he's not wearing makeup, and he can't pretend she's anything but a woman in this light with his fingers deep inside her. But then he rolls back to her, condom in hand.

She cries out in relief, and Jack presses their foreheads together again as he rolls the condom on, chest rising and falling madly.

"Yes?" he asks breathlessly, sliding his cock through the wetness between her thighs.

"Yes, yes," Hannah says, lifting her leg again to settle on his hip, arching her neck as the wide head of his cock pushes into her. She feels the stretch like a burn, can't stop moaning as he moves in and in and in.

"Jesus, you're—you're big," she hisses, and feels the welcome rumble of his laugh against her throat.

"Sweet talker," he murmurs, but there is a tightness in his voice, and his breathing is uneven.

"You feel—just—you feel..." Hannah can't finish that thought. She's going to feel him in her teeth tomorrow, and he isn't even fully seated yet. "Wait, just a second, wait."

He stops moving, breathing through clenched teeth, and Hannah leans forward, licks those teeth before she can lose her nerve. He opens his mouth and they kiss, and Hannah says, "Okay," around his tongue, feels him thrust shallowly inside her, hitting something that lights her up like Christmas. She makes the world's most embarrassing noise, but fuck it, she doesn't care if he'll only do it again. He pulls back, almost withdraws entirely, before thrusting sharply in, and this time they both make the world's most embarrassing noise, so that's okay.

Every inch of him is a shock; Hannah can't stop pushing her hips forward to take more, running her hands through his hair and over his skin. He was right—this *is* mad—and yet she's giving in to it. There is a fine trail of dark hair on his stomach, and she wants to lick her tongue across it, suck and bite and leave a million marks. She wants his cock inside her, and she wants it in her mouth. She wants him in a dress and lipstick, and she wants him naked and dark-circled in the early morning.

"Climb on top of me," Jack says softly, rolling onto his back and pulling her with him. The change in position makes his cock feel deeper somehow, leaves Hannah rolling her hips and burning up with lust. She can't help but cry out in time with each thrust, the sounds forced from his cock to her throat; his neighbors probably think someone is being murdered. Jack grabs her breasts with both hands, leans up and tongues at her nipples. What was slow and gentle previously has become hard and frantic. She raises and lowers herself on his cock, wanting desperately to touch herself, but knowing that as soon as she does she'll be lost. In the end, it's Jack who rubs his palms up her thighs and between her legs, thumbs against her clit until she's crying, moaning, begging him not to stop.

She comes so hard it makes her dizzy, the aftershocks going on and on until she swears she's going to die from it. Jack's hips start to jerk fast and unevenly, his hands on her hips holding her tightly in place.

"Jesus. Mother. Fucking. Christ, oh—"

There will be bruises on her hips in a few hours, but now there's nothing she can do but take it, take it. He thrusts deep, once, twice, wringing a moan from her. When he comes, it's with a strangled cry, more pain than pleasure. When he finally stills, his mouth is open, eyes closed tight with grief. Hannah got that last bit right, at least.

Jack opens his eyes. There is a fine sheen of sweat on his skin.

"That was—" he starts, but does not finish. Hannah is not sure how she would finish the sentence herself. Unexpected? Amazing? Insane?

Somehow she makes her thighs work, lifting herself enough that he can slip out of her. She feels sore and hollowed out, and it will be days before she thinks of touching herself.

"Who broke your heart?" she asks, the words a surprise to both of them.

Jack's face goes very still and tight before he smiles at her, with just the corner of his mouth. Hannah presses her lips to that corner.

The walk back to her car is silent. Hannah's ribs feel bruised, her chest like it's been punched, left of the breastbone. The only sound is the traffic rushing past, and the crunch of her shoes in the snow.

# REDISCOVERY

## Hedonist Six

Finding it stops me dead in my tracks.

In among the forgotten clothes, in the large wardrobe on the landing, this formerly prized possession had been lost to oblivion until a few seconds ago. The shiny teak still gleams invitingly, defending its secret from years of neglect.

I open it with an unsteady hand, half-expecting the treasure inside to have turned to dust. Yet in between the blood-red tissue paper, the black-leather-effect harness I had bought so many years ago looks like it did the day it was new. The purple detachable dildo also seems in mint condition. *Of course it is; it's never been used.*

I sit down in between piles of garments strewn around the floor: to keep, to give away, to decide later. But I've stopped caring about my earlier clear-out project in favor of gazing inside the box, reliving fantasies that have long since faded.

Years ago, when our love was still fresh and impulsive, I'd had a crazy idea. I'd wanted to turn the tables on our sex life, to see what things would be like from his perspective. For one night,

I'd be in charge, and Gary would be on his hands and knees in front of me. So I spent a few evenings researching quietly on the computer, while he was in the living room watching TV. That same week, I found the perfect strap-on for beginners: not too thick, with a secure and easy-to-wear harness. Then, of course, I'd chickened out of my plan's execution at the last moment and hidden the evidence.

Since then, we'd had a trial separation, a tearful reconciliation and wedding, adopted two dogs and gained some pounds. We'd survived doubts, suspicions, conflicting dreams and a few near-affairs. We'd moved on from screwing each other on every surface of the house—suitable or not—to bedroom sex on the weekends. I don't remember the last time Gary ordered me to my knees and took me from behind, so the idea of doing that to him could not be more alien.

I stroke the purple silicone, following the veiny texture along the shaft, up to the smooth head. Was it possible that years of quiet yet content boredom in the bedroom would add up to bringing out this crazy old plan and putting it into action? I shake my head and snap the box shut again. What a stupid idea. Although...

There's no harm in *trying it on,* is there?

Getting up, I discard my jeans and panties with the mess on the floor and take the dildo out of the box, weighing it in my hand. It's not very big at all, a perfect step up for someone who's only ever been fingered; that's what the saleslady had said, anyway. The harness feels rough on the outside, but the inside has a pleasant velvety finish. I slip it on and adjust the straps, which thankfully allow for the extra width the years have brought to my hips. When I'm satisfied that it's secure, I slide the dildo into its holder and admire my new look from above.

There's a full-length mirror in the entrance hall, so I make my way there, stripping completely naked in the process. My reflection looks powerful: it's still me, including the saggy, flabby bits I've come to hate, but with an erection. I close my hand around it and shut my eyes. I imagine it's a sad excuse for how it feels to be a man, but it's the closest I'll ever get. And I'm enjoying it.

Still stroking, I wonder about the look on Gary's face if he caught me like this. Would he be shocked, excited, offended? Perhaps I've always been the submissive one because somehow this symbol, this *weapon* he wields naturally, has made me so. But now I've got one too, and I'm ready to duel for control.

If Gary walked in on me now, I'd straighten my back, puff up my chest and order him to strip. I'd forget my insecurities, because such things don't matter when you have one of these between your legs. He'd get the bottle of lube from the bedroom, for his own benefit. I'd want him on all fours on top of the clothes I'd planned to give to charity, or better yet, on the carpet in front of the large mirror.

Yes, it would be so good to be able to see his face, as well as his ass, when I enter him.

He's always loved finger action on his prostate, whether during a wank or a blow job, and I've been happy to oblige. Lately though, there haven't been many blow jobs and his occasional morning release has consisted of good old-fashioned missionary, with me still too sleepy to care.

But this—this wouldn't be a morning quickie! This would have to be perhaps on a Saturday afternoon, when there's no rush to finish before work and no laundry to be done. No charity collection to gather up unwanteds for while he's out at soccer practice.

With Gary on his knees, ass high up and cheeks spread, I'd tease him first with my finger. I'd dab on some lube and slip and slide around the puckered ring of his entrance, which would try its best to keep me out initially. Perhaps I'd give him some encouragement with my other hand, reaching around to find his already throbbing cock. He'd be begging me to touch it, not lightly, but to grab hold and do it the way he would. Determined, a bit rough even.

The moment I'd close my fingers around his erection, he'd twitch and sigh in that way he's always done. Back when we were at it daily like bunny rabbits, and even now for our weekly morning routine, his enthusiasm toward feeling my hands on his junk hasn't waned. So why have we slipped into this tedious routine? It's my fault. I've let it become boring, because my excitement has faded as much as I feel my looks have.

I open my eyes again and focus once more on the purple cock sticking out from my groin. With my back straight, I'm obviously still chubbier than I'd want to be, but does it really matter? Does he mind? I know he says he doesn't, and that in his eyes I'm still as beautiful as I've always been, but I've been unconvinced for years.

I turn sideways to appreciate the length of the strap-on combined with the fullness of my breasts. It's surprising how feminine I look, despite this ultimate symbol of masculinity right in the center of it.

Perhaps after the initial fingering and little warm-up wank, Gary would start to ask for more. I'd want him to. I could tease him with the head of the dildo, pressing against his anus to see if he'd lean in or away from me. If he leans in, I'll know he's ready.

Squeezing more lube into my hand, I'd coat my silicone cock until it was slick. I'd spread his ass more and slowly enter. It would be hard; his body would involuntarily fight me at first. He'd have to will his muscles to relax, but once I'm in, the most difficult part would be over. I'd grab hold of his hips, like he would do to me in a similar position. And I'd push, in and out, slowly and gently at first, all the while reading his responses. The buildup would be gradual, figuring out how best to move.

Women's hips aren't made to thrust like men's are; it's bound to require practice. I wonder if he'd prefer me to continue jerking him off, or perhaps he'd try the contortionist's approach of reaching down while balancing on one hand.

How long could he last?

As my fantasy progresses, my fingers embark on a journey of exploration of their own. My breasts have swollen, my nipples tensed up. The underside of the harness is soaking up the sweetly scented juices that have started to flow ever since I allowed my mind to wander. The clenched sensation in my lower abdomen builds while I tease myself mentally as well as physically.

It's been so long since I've been this turned on, all because of this wooden box and the former secret within. The wardrobe in the hall might not be the best place for it, but at least it's secure where he won't accidentally find it. Maybe this is just what I need. I shall keep the image of him on all fours in the back of my mind for the next time we have one of our clumsy morning fucks. Maybe one day I'll tell him about it, once I've gathered the nerve. Or maybe not.

So lost am I in my reverie that I don't hear the click of the lock in time. By the time the door has swung open and Gary fills the frame, I have no opportunity to flee.

"What the..." His mouth is agape and he's dropped the bag containing his soccer kit on the floor.

"I...oh shit." As I'm trying desperately but failing to hide my modesty with both arms, the blood starts to rush into my cheeks until they glow. So much for my earlier fantasy of standing proud and ordering him around. I'm about to turn and run to safety, when he grabs me by the arm.

"I didn't know you had one of those."

"I didn't either," I respond. "I mean, I had forgotten all about it."

His eyes don't leave me for a second while he reaches behind himself to shut the door. The tension between us is electric; his fingers singe my skin. It hits me that this is the first time in a long while that I've stood in front of him fully naked. In bright, unforgiving daylight.

A devious little smile appears on his lips and his gaze focuses on the surprise addition to my anatomy. My heart continues to race as earlier daydreams come flooding back to me.

"Had I known..." As he whispers those little words in my ear, the tickle of his breath gives me goose bumps.

My body has started to read his thoughts before my mind is able to process them, and I find myself with my shoulders pushed back, like they should've been all along. With the next surge of confidence, I rest my hands on my hips and return his stare. Indeed now it's more fun *because* he didn't know.

"Strip and get down on your knees!"

"Yes, Ma'am," Gary says, unbuttoning his jeans.

# A PROVEN
# THERAPEUTIC
# FACT

## D. L. King

So, tell me Mr. Hendricks, where does it hurt most?"

My client, James Hendricks, lay stretched out, naked, on my portable, padded, black-vinyl-topped massage table in the middle of his living room. You know, they call these tables "portable" but they really aren't that easy to "port." Mr. Hendricks had helped me hoist the thing out of my car and lug it into his house but, as he carried it up the last step to the front door, I could see him wincing. I knew he was in pain.

James Hendricks had a very high-powered job that created an inordinate amount of stress in his life. I had no idea what he did but, whatever it was, it allowed him this beautiful home and those indispensable little luxuries, like my services.

I'd moved out to the West Coast to be the next big thing but was smart enough to get training in something in addition to acting. An actor's body is her instrument—well, her body and her voice—but I suppose my body is such a big part of my craft, when looking at temporary careers to fill in and pay the rent while waiting for my big break, I naturally drifted to massage school.

"Well, I guess it's a tie between my lower back and my shoulders. Sorry, Alice. I don't mean to make your life so difficult, it's just been a long week. But I know you can fix it. You always work wonders." Mr. Hendricks lay on his stomach, atop several layers of sheets, with his face in the cradle, awaiting my touch. A sheet discreetly covered his naked body.

Becoming licensed as a massage therapist was, possibly, the best thing I'd ever done. Sure, I get the occasional commercial and a line or two on a TV show every once in a while, and they pay well, don't get me wrong, but they don't exactly pay the rent. My massage business, on the other hand, quite easily covers the rent and keeps me in kibble, so to speak. It's all word of mouth, really. I work on some of the wealthiest bodies in LA, and they all seem to know each other. I guess they meet at big charity functions and schmooze with each other while walking their dogs in Bel Air. I'm discreet and I make a point *never* to work on anyone in the business; I don't need any conflicts of interest between my two careers.

Mr. Hendricks moaned when I began kneading his shoulders. I'd rolled the sheet down to his waist and was standing at his head. I could feel the knots; the poor guy really was a mess. After a while, they began to break up and I could move down his right arm. I worked both of his arms before returning to his back and slowly worked out the smaller tensions I found at his core. Saving his lower back and buttocks for later, I worked on his legs and feet to much *oooing* and *aaahing* before returning to the problem area.

There was a lot of wincing as I began to work out the knots above his hips, and some real "Ow's" when I began to work on his rear.

"All right, I'll tell you what. Let's save that for later, shall we? Why don't you roll over for me now?" I held the side of the sheet up so he could turn over without getting caught in the linens and he scooted down and turned over. I replaced the sheet and started again at the top of his body, working out the stiffness in his chest and arms, then jumped down to his legs and made my way up to his groin.

I know what you're thinking and, no, I'm not one of *those* kinds of masseuses. Well, not like you're thinking, anyway. No, as I said before, I'm an honest-to-god licensed massage therapist. I don't do lingam and yoni massages. But, nevertheless, Mr. Hendricks started to squirm when I got to that area. I could see a definite bulge in the sheet begin to appear—a bulge that hadn't been there only moments before.

"Oh, Alice, oh. Oh my god, if you could just move a little closer in. Just...a...little...closer. Oh, Alice." Mr. Hendricks began to wiggle on the table and strain his pelvic area toward me. "Alice, you're so good at what you do. I bet if you just touched it...just a little...."

"Mr. Hendricks!" I removed my hands and backed away from the table. "You know better than that! That's very naughty and you know I can't just let it go. No. Get off the table, right now," I commanded.

"No, Alice, I'm sorry, I won't do it again. Please don't make me," he said.

"No, Mr. Hendricks, I'm afraid not. I simply can't let it go. Now get up and turn around."

When I ripped the sheet off him I could see his cock at full attention. He's one of those. Not all my clients get hard or wet. Some don't get aroused at all. But Mr. Hendricks always gets hard and stays that way.

He slid off the table, cock waving in the air, but I noticed him wince when his feet hit the ground and again when he stood up straight. He really was in a lot of pain.

"Brace yourself, Mr. Hendricks; you know how to do it." He placed his hands on the edge of the table and moved back a bit, leaning forward. "Spread those legs. You know better than that!" He complied and once he was in position, I began to scold.

"Just how do you think that makes me feel, Mr. Hendricks?" I asked. I smacked his right buttcheek. "I'm no cheap floozy!" I smacked his left buttcheek. "Do you think I'm some sort of whore, Mr. Hendricks?" I peppered both sides of his bottom with hard spanks.

"No, no, I'm sorry, Alice. I don't think of you that way at all, you know I don't. I swear! I just can't help it. You're so beautiful and, well, you know guys; we're just sort of built that way. It happens. I can't help it. Please, Alice!"

I had continued to spank him throughout his apology. "I don't believe you, Mr. Hendricks. I don't think you see me as a trained professional. I'm afraid I'm going to have to teach you some respect!" By this time, his bottom was a nice, uniform pink, but it would need to get a lot pinker, perhaps even closer to red, before I could move on to the next phase of relieving Mr. Hendricks's pain. I slowed my spanks but brought my hand down harder, alternating cheeks to a chorus of squeals and moans and groans, with plenty of "yummy" sounds thrown in.

Mr. Hendricks was a *spanko*, as are many of my clients. Mr. Hendricks loved to be spanked. For him, spanking was sexual, although it wasn't necessarily so for many of my other clients. Regardless of whether it was sexual or not, spanking helped to relieve tension for some people.

As I said, my client base had grown through word of mouth and a very special subset of my client base, also grown through word of mouth, relied on my expertise as both a massage therapist and a powerful spanking top. For those clients, spanking helped to release muscle tension and allowed for deeper relaxation. I provided therapy based on the client's needs and experience.

Mr. Hendricks liked it hard. In fact, a gentle spanking, rather than loosening him up, could exacerbate his already painfully cramped muscles. I always got a workout with Mr. Hendricks, but he really needed it today.

"You stay right where you are," I said. "Don't you move an inch." I walked over to my bag and brought out several implements. Since he hadn't moved, and therefore didn't see what was going on, there was a great, excited cry when I smacked his left buttock with my large, leather paddle. My spanks were measured and slow, alternating sides, positioned over the plumpest area of his bottom—the area just above the curve toward his thighs. Keeping the paddle pressed against his skin, after each initial smack, helped to intensify and deepen the pain of the blow. It was that kind of deep pain that would help him to loosen up.

By now, his skin was a dark rose, but I knew he needed more. I replaced the leather paddle with a Lucite one. This produced a much sharper sensation. I spent another ten minutes of solid spanking time with this paddle, covering his entire bottom and ending with a few swats against the crease between his bottom and his thighs, a particularly painful area. All during the spanking, I berated him for his supposed disrespect, knowing this would also help to relax him.

Fairly certain he was ready, I said, "Mr. Hendricks, I know just how naughty you are. I don't want to see it so don't you dare turn around. You march right into the bathroom and take care of yourself so I can finish your massage." Like I said earlier, I'm not that kind of masseuse and I couldn't very well complete the massage with his raging hard-on. Besides, an orgasm would help to relax him that much more, and this was the pattern with Mr. Hendricks.

He returned with a towel wrapped around his waist. I lifted the sheet up and in front of myself so that he could have some privacy when he dropped the towel and climbed back onto the table. "Facedown," I said.

Once he was settled, I folded the sheet down to his knees. "Sorry, Alice," he said.

His bottom was red and puffy. I placed my hands on both cheeks and felt the heat from the abraded skin. Gently, I began to knead the muscles at the top of his buttocks. I could tell they were already much less tight than they'd been before his spanking.

"How's that feel, Mr. Hendricks? Better?" There were no shrieks and fewer "Ow"s.

"Alice, it's a miracle," he sighed. "I don't know how you do it. Nobody else has ever been able to give me a massage that works. There have been times when I've ended up in even more pain than I was in at the beginning. But never with you. If I weren't already married, I'd propose."

Of course I knew how I did it. But still, his words made me smile.

I continued to knead and stretch the muscles in his lower back and butt and after another fifteen minutes, I could tell he was feeling much better.

The secret was the spanking. It's a proven therapeutic fact. At least, I've proven it, with my special clients. And the evidence was plain to see, where Mr. Hendricks was concerned: it stopped the noises in his head; it centered him; it stimulated his circulation; it was *good* pain and that made the endorphins flow. It was like running for an athlete. It took his mind off the *bad* pain, which let me, at least temporarily, fix the damage his very stressful life had caused.

I'm not even sure he realized what was happening. Of course he knew he was getting a spanking, and that he wanted that spanking, but I don't think he equated it with the massage. I think, for Mr. Hendricks, it had become about his misbehavior and subsequent punishment. Most of my other spankophile clients recognized it as part of their therapy. But whether they understood that or not, they were getting what they needed. The thing is, I can't stand to see people in pain and I'll do whatever it takes to help them, regardless of how they perceive it. After all, it was, at least in part, what my special clients hired me for.

After the massage, I let him relax on the table for a bit while I put away my oils, lotions and spanking implements. I left the room and gave him time to get up and dress in private. I returned with a glass of water to find him standing by the table with a big grin on his face. I handed him the glass and reminded him to drink plenty of water to flush out the toxins the massage had coaxed from his muscles.

I wouldn't let him help me pack up my table or carry it out to the car. I didn't want to risk negating any of the gains he'd made, but I was happy to see the spring in his step as he walked me out and waved goodbye.

"See you in a week, Alice?"

"Sure thing, Mr. Hendricks."

Who am I kidding? He knew exactly what he was getting.

# CAUGHT

## Rei Pardieu

A ll right. If you want to be treated like a dog so badly, I'll grant your wish."

Those were the words I heard from directly behind me as I sat looking at my computer screen. I froze in place and glanced over my shoulder toward my Sir, who had an unreadable expression on his face. My cheeks were flushed red with embarrassment as I considered closing the tab on the manga I was reading, but I knew it was already too late. Leo had been watching me as I'd gotten more excited by the scenario before me—two girls dressed in nothing but bikinis and limb restraints barking and chasing a ball for their Master.

It was humiliating to be caught so directly; I wanted to protest but he knew me too well to listen to me in these situations. It's always been this way from the start of our relationship; if there was something that I was curious about I would spend hours on the Internet seeking it out and he, my Sir, would watch the whole time to see what had piqued my interest. Then, when I least expected it, he would whisper my desires into my ear and chuckle as I went red.

Today was different though. Usually he waited until I was no longer on the computer before mentioning his plans. The fact that he seemed as eager as I was excited me, but it also made me a little worried. We didn't own any of the limb restraints that were used in this kind of play, and it made me wonder what Sir had in store for me.

I didn't have long to think about it, though, as he leaned over and grasped me by the D-ring of the collar I was wearing. A sharp tug had me half out of the chair, balanced shakily on the tips of my toes and panting softly in arousal. Sir grinned as his other hand smoothed over the dress I was wearing and grasped firmly at my crotch.

"It's so warm down here, Lily," he cooed, pulling my face closer to his. "I think you need to take everything off." The finger looped into my collar slowly uncurled from the metal as he lowered his hand and guided my feet to stand flat on the floor. As soon as I was steady, he used the collar to tilt up my chin and look into my eyes as his other hand withdrew from between my thighs, his fingers making sure to brush past my clitoris on their way. I shivered and tried not to break eye contact as I gave a weak nod in response. "Good girl."

He stepped back from me as he uttered my favorite words and gestured at my dress with a flick of his wrist. Almost instantly, I reached down and pulled it up over my head before holding it awkwardly in my hands. I resisted the urge to toss it to the floor like I had done so many times in the past, instead attempting to fold it the way Sir liked with my shaking hands. It was very difficult to do since I was so nervous and aroused that I couldn't quite remember the exact way he liked it, but I managed somehow. As he looked at me with a smirk, I turned to put it on the chair behind me, knowing he was observing every inch of my body. Even without looking I knew my nipples would be stiff and my blue knickers noticeably wet. He could probably see the shape of my pussy through the material; that thought aroused me further.

When I turned back to look at him again, he simply gestured toward my underwear without saying a word. The look of impatience on his face told me he was annoyed that he needed to remind me. I took a deep breath and moved my hands down to my hips, slipping my thumbs under the waistband and dragging the offending panties to my knees without a second thought. I looked down as I began to lift my leg out and blushed deeply as I saw the wet patch staining my underwear. It was much bigger than I thought it would be, plus I knew he must have seen everything.

It wasn't the first time he'd seen me naked and it certainly wouldn't be the last, yet I still found it difficult to get used to. Sir was the first partner who had really taken an interest in looking at me properly instead of just trying to fuck me. It would be strange if I had gotten used to it by now.

With the last of my clothing gone, Sir smiled.

"I want you to wait in the living room." Sir paused as I frowned slightly in confusion, then added, "But you'd better go there on your hands and knees."

The latter part of the instruction was understandable, but I couldn't wrap my head around the fact that he wanted me in the living room. Usually he tried to keep this sort of thing in the bedroom or the bathroom where no one else could see. Our living room has massive balcony windows overlooking the neighborhood behind us; he generally opted to make sure we wouldn't be observed.

I was drawn out of these worries by the sound of Sir clicking his tongue impatiently. I hurriedly moved to my knees, looking up at him from my position on the floor. I waited just long enough to see his smile return, then shuffled my way across the floor, making sure to keep my ankles in the air behind me. As I passed by his legs, he gave me a firm slap on the ass to hurry me up and followed me out into the hall.

He said nothing but I knew he was watching me closely, so I crawled to the living room as he'd instructed. My heart was beating madly in my chest but I did my best to ignore it as I pushed the door with both of my hands. I heard him chuckle— appreciatively, I hoped—and then the sound of the bedroom door closing. The living room door shut behind me not a moment later.

From the angle I was at, I soon noticed two bowls lined up neatly on the kitchen floor and went over to investigate them. I didn't dare get up now in case Sir returned so I ended up staring down into the bowls from my position on the floor. As expected, one was filled halfway with water but the other was empty. I wondered what he might put in the bowl. Would it be real dog food? Dry or wet? Would he really make me eat it?

The familiar slam of the living room door drew me out of my thoughts and I jumped a little in surprise. My long brown hair slipped from my shoulder and splashed into the water with little warning, getting some on my arm and onto the floor. From the doorway, Sir sighed and put down the bag of things he had brought in with him, striding over to me faster than I could think.

His hand bunched in the hair at the back of my head as he pushed my face toward the now-wet floor. "Come on, Lily. Lick it up."

His tone of voice left no room for discussion. Though I was a little worried about how clean the place was, I flicked my tongue out. As I lapped at the puddle I noticed him kneeling down beside me, his face studying mine, though I could only see him from the corner of my eye. It took every ounce of will-power I had not to turn to look directly at him. I knew he wouldn't want me to and the hand in my hair would hurt if I did, but the desire to know what expression he was wearing was almost overpowering. Instead I just kept licking until the floor was pretty dry, the shine of my spit against the wood the only remainder of my mess. I was left a bit breathless from the exercise and could feel my chest heave as I sucked in as much air as I could.

The hand in my hair slowly loosened as Sir's face disappeared from my peripheral vision. After a moment of just feeling the weight on the back of my head it moved and began to stroke down my neck and over my spine. I heard a murmur of approval from behind me as I felt a squeeze on my left buttcheek.

"You can put your tongue away now."

It took a few seconds for what he said to register in my mind and I immediately closed my mouth in embarrassment. I hadn't realized I had left it hanging out like that, panting, and I felt suddenly ashamed. What must I look like, naked with my tongue lolling out of my mouth like an animal? Surely anyone who saw me would think me ridiculous! I stiffened up at the thought of Sir laughing at me from behind. What if this was a bad idea? What if he thought less of me for acting this way? The idea was unbearable.

The squeeze on my bum suddenly turned into a sharp smack. I jumped in surprise. My head snapped around to where Sir was standing, my eyes seeking his face to see what he was thinking even though I was afraid of what I would find. I didn't expect to see a smile shining back at me. The tender look on his face was confusing but soothing at the same time. He looked like he was enjoying himself, though I couldn't be totally sure. I stared at the serene expression for what felt like an eternity, only coming out of my trance when his lips moved and he spoke.

"Lower your head and lift your ass up for me."

I blinked, then lowered my head obediently to the floor as I pushed my strength down into my knees. My bum lifted off the floor as high as I could get it without getting to my feet. It stuck out behind me and I shivered as I felt cool air against my wet, exposed pussy. Was this what he wanted?

It must have been, because the next moment Sir slid a finger into me, teasing me as the fingertip rubbed against my wet insides. I held back a murmur and arched my back more, trying to make it reach that special spot that felt so good. Sir chuckled behind me and slipped his finger out, tracing over my perineum lightly before pressing it firmly against my asshole. I couldn't help but push my hips back against him, but just as I felt the tip penetrate me, he pulled it away. Frustrated, I almost lifted my head to complain when I felt him smear something cold and wet over my anus instead.

Lube.

While Sir and I have tried anal sex in the past, it isn't a common part of our sex life. For one thing, it always requires more lube and patience than either of us have to spare at the time and for another, it never feels all that great to either of us anyway. Sir says he always prefers my pussy because it is a little looser and easier to move around in and I have always been happy with that. Anal really hasn't been something I've thought about all that much—until now.

Before I could truly react to his teasing ministrations, one of his fingers pushed inside my ass. The burning sensation from the stretching caused me to flush hot with arousal; I could swear I felt my own juices trickle out of my pussy and drip down my thighs. It was difficult to remember the last time I'd been this turned on.

Sir slowly pumped his finger in and out of me, causing me to shiver and try to muffle my moans against the flooring. It was embarrassing to enjoy his fingers there, to know he could see every inch of my most private areas and do whatever he wanted to them. I wouldn't stop him—I never would. I wanted this so much that it felt like I was going to explode if he didn't fuck me now. This was why I was no good when it came to anal—I just wanted everything straightaway. I'd suffer the consequences later.

Fortunately, it seemed that Sir agreed with my desire to hurry along as he slipped his finger out and then pressed something else against my ass. Was it his cock? I wasn't sure; it felt cold and smooth, so that wouldn't make sense but I didn't know if I cared. I couldn't help but eagerly push back onto it, letting out a gasp as Sir pushed it forward at the same time and then it was buried inside me. I squeezed down on it hard and lifted my body slightly to try and get a look at him from underneath.

The sight that greeted me took my breath away.

Between my legs, all I saw was a long, fluffy black tail. I couldn't tell what it was made from but it looked like real fur. I squeezed down on the toy inside me again and the tail moved slightly. I thought it must be a butt plug and from the weight and smoothness I was willing to bet that it was made of glass. I didn't remember us ever having used this toy before and I didn't think Sir had ever discussed the idea with me either. I wanted to speak but didn't know what to say.

Luckily it seemed my opinion wasn't wanted, nor was it needed.

Sir pushed firmly on the butt plug and used his thumb to make it curve around inside my body. As the fluffy tail brushed the insides of my thighs, I couldn't help but sigh happily at the ticklish feeling.

"That's a good girl," Sir murmured. His fingers splayed out on either side of the plug and spread me open a little wider. "Now, let's see about playing fetch, shall we?" He didn't need to convince me. In my enthusiasm, I barked loudly and wiggled my butt in Sir's face to make the tail sway side to side. He chuckled and gave me another slap on the ass. "Get up and face me then, girl."

When I turned around, I saw a tennis ball in his hand, another item I didn't know we owned but was very happy to see. I knelt up as high as I could and held my hands to my chest as though they were paws. The look of satisfaction on Sir's face spurred me on as I barked again, trying to ignore how silly I felt. He lifted his hand high and looked squarely at my face as he made a throwing motion. My eyes latched on to his hand and watched intensely as the ball did not leave it. There was a pause and then I looked back at his face, surprised to see how full of mirth it was.

"Clever girl!" I wiggled my bum some more and let out another bark as he moved over to stroke the sides of my face. His warm hands felt great on my skin. I looked up into his eyes, adoring every single thing about him. He smiled back down at me and kissed me on the forehead. "All right, now let's actually play fetch." He stepped back and threw the ball to the corner of the room, laughing as I dashed over on my knees to grab it with my mouth. I returned it by dropping it at his feet and he threw it again, playing a back-and-forth game that seemed to go on forever.

After twenty minutes, when I was lying on the floor exhausted and sweaty, Sir decided the game of fetch was over. He carefully guided my head back to the water bowl and I gratefully lapped the water up, closing my eyes in bliss at how cool and refreshing the liquid felt on my tongue. My body ached all over and my knees hurt from being on the floor so long but I wouldn't have had it any other way. I was as happy as the kinky characters from my manga. I sighed contentedly while he soothed his hands up and down my back as I drank. The gesture was affectionate and loving—until his fingertips grasped my ass and pulled me up into a kneeling position. I was too lethargic to protest as his thumbs teased the outside of my pussy. To my surprise, I was still wet. He roughly rubbed a thumb over my clit and I moaned deeply, choking a little on the water in my mouth. I couldn't believe I was still so turned on but there was no fighting it as he rubbed me again and made my knees feel weak.

My face pressed against the cool floor as he started to finger my clit more insistently. With just a few strokes of his fingers, I climaxed, much faster than usual, but I was so much more aroused today that it was easy. I tried not to moan again because I wanted him to keep going but Sir knew my body too well and smacked me on the butt for not making a sound. As part of our dynamic, I'm always supposed to vocalize my orgasms; I knew I was in trouble for breaking that rule.

Without saying a word, he flipped the tickly tail upward so it rested on my back before pulling his pants down. I shook in anticipation and pushed my body back toward him as I felt the head of his cock against my sodden pussy, forcing the tip inside. Instead of chastising me like he usually would, Sir grabbed my hips and pulled me back onto his dick, impaling me deep and rough, just the way I like it. I cried out from pleasure and he thrust into me again as one of his hands grasped the base of the butt plug and wriggled it around inside me. The sensation of both his cock and the plug plunging into me at once was amazing. I squeezed hard on his cock to let him know how much I appreciated it, and he did it again, his ragged breaths audible for once.

Those rough noises emanating from him made me want to please him even more. I squirmed back onto him, clenching around his cock in the rhythmic motions that never fail to make him burst inside me. I wanted him to come; I longed to feel the pulsing of his penis as he shot his load and the weight of his body against my back as he caught his breath. I had already felt so good today that my own pleasure didn't matter anymore. I wanted this to be all about Sir. His hand reached underneath us to toy with my clitoris. It only took two strokes between his fingers before I was screaming, the whole world seeming to flash behind my eyelids. In the haze of my orgasm I felt his cock pulsing inside me. His body urged mine to the floor as he pushed as hard against me as he could.

When I came back to myself I realized that Sir was still inside me, his hands moving up and down my chest and stomach affectionately. It felt like playtime was over but I didn't say anything yet, waiting for his signal that I could speak. I didn't want to end this if Sir was not ready to and I felt as though a single word would ruin everything. His lips brushed the back of my neck and his breath tickled my ear.

"Was that fun, Lily?" His voice was shaky but affectionate. Just hearing it soothed me. I nodded in response. He chuckled softly and cuddled me tighter. "I'm pleased to hear that. You've been a very good girl." My chest swelled with pride and I tilted my head back so I could kiss him, enjoying the soft press of his warm mouth.

"Thank you, Sir."

A few comfortable moments passed by before he pulled away and slipped the butt plug out of my sore yet satisfied body. As he put his pants back on properly I got up on my knees, sitting in the position he prefers as I waited for further instructions. I could feel the evidence of his orgasm dripping out onto the floor but I paid it no mind, just like he'd taught me.

"Do you think you can keep being a good girl for your Sir?" This wasn't really a question. He knew I would always say yes and do whatever he asked of me. I love him so much. Leo leaned down and put the tail into my hands. "Please go and wash this properly in the sink and then clean up the mess you're making on my floors. After that, I'll see you back in the office." I nodded and watched as he left the living room before I got to my feet and rushed over to the sink to make sure the new toy stayed beautiful.

My mind flickered back to how nervous I'd been about being caught and I laughed softly at myself as I began to run the water from the tap.

I couldn't wait for him to discover what I planned to look at next.

# JANE'S FANTASY, YOUR FANTASY

## Annabeth Leong

*J*ane

This was supposed to be Jane's fantasy, but now you're the one living it. You're not sure exactly how that switch occurred—maybe you should have kept your mouth shut when she proposed her idea to you and Rob.

Feeling a bit foolish, you follow the script the three of you worked out, stripping naked outside the bathroom door, folding your clothes carefully and hiding them away in the linen closet. You feel intermingled with Jane, knowing that this could easily have been her standing where you are now, a curl of anxiety in the pit of her stomach, a chill from the air settling into her skin. Since the three of you got together, you have been entranced by the fluidity of the boundaries between you. Sometimes in bed it's as if Jane's cunt is your own, but the same goes for Rob's cock. Often you close your eyes and allow yourself to float between the two, as if your body is an ocean wrapping around their two definite and opposite forms.

You run your hands down the front of your bare chest and

tweak your nipples, thinking of Jane's heavy breasts.

She's waiting for you in the bathroom, which she has gotten overly serious about decorating to look like a temple. LED candles line every surface, and the scent of amber rises from the bathwater she has prepared. Flowers cover the mirror on the front of the medicine cabinet, making the room seem darker. Some of the strange trinkets she likes to buy are in here, too, though you've never been clear on what the twisted metal forms are supposed to represent. You suppress your smile because you don't want to offend her.

Jane kneels beside the tub wearing nothing but a shawl wrapped around her hips, a flower in her hair and a set of clamps swinging from her breasts. You find the whole scene a bit silly, but that doesn't stop your body from responding to hers. The dim light flickers off the water and makes her skin seem even warmer than you know it is. She gives you a mysterious expression from beneath a fringe of dark hair and stands, the chain between her breasts clinking as she does. Her curves go far beyond the obvious. Of course you admire the lovely arcs of breasts and hips and thighs, but Jane has the abundance of a fertility goddess, and she is also soft and round in her calves, her stomach, her fingers.

You notice that you're thinking about goddesses and can't stop the smile that comes now. As usual, Jane has managed to pull you into her world.

Her lips twitch as well, reminding you that she does have a sense of humor about her ways. "Are you ready for your purification, initiate?"

You've forgotten your line. Instead, with an inarticulate sound, you step into her arms.

She envelops you. Her palms are damp from the bathwater. Pressing against you, her nipples are warm and tight, and the clamps cold and hard. She touches you methodically, fingertips brushing your forehead, lips, throat, navel and inner thighs. You agreed to these ritualistic touches because you wanted to make her happy, but they have begun to take on significance even if you don't know exactly what they mean. The beginnings of arousal take root in the depths of your pelvis.

"Tonight, in this place, you will claim the pleasures of the body. You will do so on your own terms, but know that I will be beside you." Jane intones the words with the dramatic voice of a movie villain. You cough to cover an involuntary nervous laugh. She frowns, but goes on. "The first step is to leave behind all that is old so that your body may become new. We will wash away the past."

She says this with a type of gentleness you've never been comfortable with because it makes you wish that you could cry. You've been open with Jane and Rob as you have with no other lovers, and for a moment you regret how much you told them about the things that have happened in your life and the ways that your body and desires have made you feel afraid and ashamed. That, after all, is how you got into this situation. Jane told you both about her fantasy of being taken as if for the first time, and when you reacted to it, she and Rob decided it would be better to design the scene for you.

You look away from her, searching for something bland to focus on, but she has transformed the bathroom too thoroughly and you can't escape her intentions. In desperation, you recall the chocolate you ate in the break room at work earlier that day and other mundane details. She seems to know that you've pulled away and waits until you have a hold of yourself before guiding you into the bath.

The water feels more intimate than ordinary water. Its heat rolls between the cheeks of your ass, reminding you where Jane's ritual is headed. You shiver, and it's only the pressure of Jane's hands that allows you to complete the process of entering the water.

She bathes you at first by scooping handfuls of water and pouring them over you, but as you begin to crave her touch, she gives that to you. Jane's oiled fingers smooth across your skin, smelling of coconut and sugar. You sink farther into the warmth and steam and sensation. As if you've had a glass of heady wine, your thoughts lift and drift, no longer quite sensible.

Jane doesn't caress you in an overtly sensual way, but as the bath continues, you notice yourself twitching with arousal. If the script for this scene allowed, you would pull her close and bury your face between her pussy lips, but you know she wouldn't like for you to break the spell that way. You absorb her touch and try to contain the desire it builds within you.

## How You Got into This

Rob came in Jane's ass and collapsed onto her with a grunt. You were under them both, your fingers on Jane's clit and your tongue in her mouth. Until that moment, you'd been caught up in the intimate voyeurism of your position, rocked by Rob's thrusts, privy to the way Jane's cunt clenched in response to him. Their bodies were heavy, though, and the difficulty of breathing with both of them on top of you snapped you out of your sensual haze. You released Jane and began working your way into a free spot on the bed.

Jane sighed and clung to you. "Don't move yet." Her voice was thick. "Everything's too perfect right now." She nibbled the side of your neck. "I love you. And Rob, I love you, too. Jesus, I love you both."

Rob squeezed her, the gesture transferring through her body to yours. "It was good." He made no move to pull out of her ass.

"I want..." Jane often spent her postcoital moments fantasizing about what she wanted to try next, and you and Rob shared a knowing smile. "It would be so hot to take it in the ass as if it was the first time."

The derisive snort came out of you before you realized it would hurt her feelings. Her head snapped in your direction. "What?" you demanded, your guilt at having insulted her making you defensive.

She continued to stare at you. Rob raised an eyebrow, urging you to make it right. You shrugged, embarrassed now. "First times are awkward, right? Doesn't make sense to go back to that." There was more behind your words, making your voice crack, and you tried again to disengage yourself, afraid that your lovers would find you out.

"Awkward can be sexy," Jane said. "It can be fun."

"Sure. I guess."

"You guess." The darkness of Rob's tone told you he already guessed some of what you wished you could conceal.

You didn't want them to touch you anymore, and they understood, gently making space for you to crawl out of contact with them. You realized it would be hopeless to try to hide. They already knew you far too well. "People pressure you, you know. I don't think I've been ready the first time I did anything." You went on a bit, oblivious to their frowns of concern. Then you noticed Jane's furrowed brow and Rob's clenched fist. "It's fine," you said quickly. "I'm fine." You were surprised that what you said upset them. You'd always assumed everyone's story was like yours and that, like you, people just didn't often talk about those things.

It was too late to downplay what you'd said, though. Jane insisted on a "redo"—giving you a first-time experience that you could treasure. Though you expected ritual from Jane, Rob was the one who designed most of the scene the three of you agreed to enact. Rob realized how much you needed to be in control, and he figured out how to accomplish that.

*Rob*

You leave the bathroom and go to the living room, which Rob has prepared. He's created a starker landscape than Jane's flowery, candlelit temple. The lights are off, and white sheets cover every irrelevant piece of furniture.

Contrast pulls your gaze where Rob wants it to be. He's thrown a red sheet over the coffee table and populated that surface with lube and stainless-steel butt plugs arranged from small to large. Beside the coffee table, on a sturdy wooden chair, a thick black dildo rises from the seat.

Rob stands beyond the dildo. You recognize his club clothes, the black mesh shirt, leather pants and studded boots, but in the context of the evening, his attire seems priestly. His dark skin blends into the room's shadows. The top of his bald head gleams in the light you've let in from the hallway, and the changes in illumination make it impossible for you to read his face.

When you enter, he doesn't look up. Instead, he waits until you become uncertain, shifting from one foot to the other and wondering if you're supposed to start in on the butt plugs with no comment from Rob. You are still warm from Jane's bath, so it's not cold that makes you shiver.

"We got enthusiastic about doing this scene," Rob says, "but I'm going to ask you now if you're sure about it. Are you happy about this? Is this what you want? Don't worry about the way Jane and I might feel. I want to know how *you* feel."

You want to be honest with him. "I wasn't sure this was necessary, but now I think there's something to it."

"Does that mean you want this? Are you ready? As far as I'm concerned, we can pack this all up and try again next week."

The butt plugs on the coffee table ask the question more boldly than he can. His cock has been in your ass plenty of times, but now he and Jane have forced you to acknowledge the squirming fear that's always present on some level, even when you're so turned on that you beg for it. You glance toward him as you hesitate, but he seems content to stand there all night if necessary.

Unable to make up your mind, you step closer to the coffee table, and then kneel. With the tip of one finger, you nudge the smallest butt plug. The way it rolls in response speaks to its perfect balance. It's surprisingly warm to your touch, and touching the side of one of the bottles of lube confirms that Rob has made sure that everything on the table is already at body temperature. The caring act makes you feel safer than you've ever been. Again, you find that you can hardly stand your lovers' gentleness.

You are more certain than ever that you can take all the time in the world to decide what you want to do. The butt plug is weighty when you lift it, more than its size would suggest. The smooth metal surface reflects hints of the room around you, including a distorted view of Rob's tall figure. You ask yourself whether you want it inside you and your body responds with a tremor of intense arousal that contrasts with the lingering relaxation of Jane's bath.

Reaching behind yourself, you explore with the tip of your finger. Your body is sensitive and receptive, and you moan aloud as you circle your asshole. "Yes," you tell Rob, your voice shaking.

"Then remember: You've never done this before. This is the first time. There is no right and wrong, and you do everything exactly the way you want at exactly the pace you want it."

You look up at him, feeling small because you're so far below him. "Okay." You don't like how timid you sound, but this, also, is honest.

Behind you, the floor creaks, and you see that Jane has followed you into the living room. Rob holds up a hand, stopping her. "We're both here to do whatever we can for you, but if you want to be alone for this…"

"No!" You stand and reach a hand toward each of them, forward and backward, balanced between them as always. "Please stay." Rob grins, and Jane nods solemnly. She sits cross-legged on the floor, casually exposing her cunt, which is bare beneath her shawl. Rob steps farther back into the shadows, but remains standing.

You close your eyes. You can feel them both, even though they're not touching you. This relationship constantly takes on unexpected shapes, always growing into more than you dared to hope for it.

An exhale guides you down to the floor again. You make everyone wait, listening to the three of you breathing. A pulse begins somewhere in the room. You convince yourself it is the sound of your heartbeats, synchronized by the ritual, sounding larger and louder than normal. You realize how much Jane's thoughts have become your thoughts in the time you've been together. Like Rob, though, you no longer have anything to prove, no need to close yourself off from her. You realize now that there are far worse things in the world than silliness and a little faith.

You keep expecting one of them to tell you to get on with it. You can't imagine it's arousing for either of them to watch you kneeling, breathing slowly in and out, the butt plug resting inert in the palm of one hand. They may have designed the scene, but the pace of it is in your hands now, just like the plug.

The moment stretches, but no matter how much you allow it to extend, you feel no tension or pressure. Your insides tighten anyway, but the sensation is benign rather than anxious. Antic-ipation.

Unexpected desire bubbles up within you, steaming off your skin like the lingering aromas of Jane's bath. The wait has been worth it, because you are certain now that you want to do this, for the reasons your lovers gave as well as a few private ones of your own.

You spread lube over the plug. Your tongue rests in the corner of your mouth as you do, a testament to your careful concentration. You are used to sex punctuated by sweating and moaning, haste and need. The quiet and serenity of this scene make you feel this must be something other than sex.

It is with a strange sense of dignity that you spread the cheeks of your ass with your left hand and set the tip of the plug against your ass with your right. You press the plug gingerly forward, expecting a long negotiation with your body. Your ass, however, swallows it smoothly, with an ease that you've never known.

You breathe and allow your mind to absorb what your body has always done. You are full inside, but feel no need to squirm or whine. You wait, weighing the sensation, asking yourself whether it feels good. There is a heaviness to the plug. Your ass twitches around it as if adjusting its grip, and in that moment inner skin glides against steel, hidden muscles clench, and with sudden, blinding clarity, you know that this is heaven and you need to come right now.

### How They Helped You Make a Selfish Plan

"And then," Jane said, "when you're ready, Rob or I can fuck your ass. When you ask, of course. Or maybe we should both do it. I could warm you up with my fingers and then guide him in."

Since the three of you got together, you have often wondered how you ever had time for television. You don't know what's on the radio anymore, and you haven't seen any of the videos people are watching on the Internet. In all your recent memories, you see the three of you, naked, sticky with sweat and sex, limbs as tangled together as your desires, insatiable, pausing your fucking only long enough to catch your breath or plan more elaborate fucking. This moment was no different. Your jaw hurt either from sucking Rob's cock or eating Jane's pussy. You'd come so hard a few minutes earlier that you'd given yourself a headache, but you weren't sorry. You traced the shape of Jane's breast over Rob's chest and tried to focus on what Jane was suggesting.

There was something about it that you didn't like, but instead of nailing down precisely what, you would rather have ignored the scene you were planning and sucked her nipples a little longer. Again, it was Rob who understood and stepped in. "No," he said, the shake of his head firm.

"No?" Jane grabbed his bare ass and teased the cheeks apart with her fingers. "I'm good at it, you know."

He grunted. "I do know."

"Come on." She grabbed your hand and guided it toward Rob's ass, next to hers. "I'll show you exactly what I'll do to you."

Rob gasped as she probed at his asshole, but then wriggled free. "No. It can't be one of us."

You laughed. "Well, it can't be anyone else. You two are the only people I want."

He touched the point of your chin. You marveled at how the gesture made you feel both challenged and protected. "If it's one of us, you'll try to please us."

"There's nothing wrong with that," you said.

"There's nothing wrong with it, but it's not what we're doing here." He sighed. "Look, let's say it's me fucking you, and you want to take it really slow. If you go too slow, my cock might start getting soft—that's just reality. Then you or Jane is trying to keep me turned on, and the scene's not about you anymore."

"If I do it and use a strap-on, that wouldn't be a problem," Jane pointed out, waggling her eyebrows.

Rob shrugged, leaving the point for you to take over if you wanted to. You smiled at Jane, but agreed with Rob. "I know what he means," you told Jane. "I wouldn't want you to get bored. I'd start moving to make the harness rub your clit. It's weird to be selfish. It's not easy."

*You*

You have the largest plug inside your ass. You have no idea how long Jane and Rob have been watching you take one plug after another, but it feels as if it's been all night. Your hand works lazily at your sex—you've already made yourself come once and, while you could get yourself going again, you don't want to masturbate just to avoid what you know is the next step.

The dildo waits in the chair where Rob has mounted it, the only lover in this room that you can fuck with total selfishness. You crawl to it, knowing that Rob and Jane are watching your ass, wondering if the silver base of the plug inside you flashes in the dim light as you move.

On a whim, you kiss the tip of the dildo when you reach it, an impromptu ritual touch of your own. Then you lube it, enjoying the long strokes of your palm down its hard surface.

You stand, keeping your eyes on the glistening phallus. A sigh escapes your lips as you remove the plug that fills your ass. Rob steps over to hold the chair steady for you. You brace your hands on the chair back, between his, and he hooks his pinkie finger around yours. The sweetness of the touch makes you look up and meet his eyes as you move forward to straddle the chair. The side of the dildo tickles your inner thigh. Your stomach flutters as you think about how it will feel to take it in.

"Do you want Jane to come close, too?" Rob whispers. You nod, wondering how he always seems to know what you want a few seconds before you do.

The chain between Jane's nipples clinks, and moments later you feel the heat of her body radiating into your back.

"Touch me," you tell her.

Her hands come to rest against your outer arms, so lightly that you can barely feel them. It's enough for you to feel joined with them both even as you perform this action that the three of you have decided must come from you alone.

You lower yourself cautiously, allowing the thick head of the dildo to spread your cheeks. A little pressure lodges it just inside your asshole. Well-opened by the plugs, you can tell that it will admit the dildo easily. You could take it all now, but you pause instead, thigh muscles trembling slightly, arm muscles twitching as they stabilize you.

You close your eyes and tease the dildo in and out of your ass. The elasticity of your own body amazes and pleases you. Your ass is slick and just tight enough for pleasure. Recalling that you are supposed to be doing this as if for the first time, you prepare to adjust your behavior, then realize you have nothing to change. This moment feels absolutely new.

Standing naked between your lovers, fucking your own ass because you all thought that would be a good idea, you don't even recognize sex anymore. This thing you're doing with Jane and Rob has its own unique form and purpose, one you could never have conceived even a few short years ago.

You throw your head back, so far that you can look at Jane. "I get this fantasy now," you tell her. You want them both to touch you more, to lick you everywhere, but you know that they'll hang back until you've had your moment with this dildo. Never have you felt so decadent or so in control of your pleasure.

You take the dildo farther into your body. You don't know if what's going on in your head matches Jane's intentions or Rob's plans, but none of that matters now. Squeezing the chair back tighter, you fuck yourself, letting your movements be wild because you know that Rob and Jane will catch you if they need to.

The last bit of pressure stored up within you explodes into joy. You seat yourself fully on the dildo, and in that moment your body is a comfortable place to live. You shift your weight and let it rest on your ass, pressing an exquisite ache into your deepest parts. Full to the brim, you feel magnanimous, ready to give and receive without boundaries or reservations. You reach for Jane's cunt and Rob's cock. Your body, his body, her body—all three mix into one pleasure.

# SELF-DENIAL

## Tilly Hunter

No, no, don't make me come."

Maybe Lewis thinks I mean "yet." Maybe he thinks it's one of those, "No, yes, no, it's too good," things. But what I mean is don't, just don't. He does anyway. He's good with his tongue. So good. He presses his face to me, chasing me as my hips rise off the bed, wringing out every last drop of orgasm, his hands on my ass pulling me to him until I collapse onto them, spent.

He drags his fingers out from under me and starts to kiss his way up my belly. His lips brush between my breasts and up to my mouth and his hard cock meets my mound.

*Yes, fuck me now,* I think, *fuck me while my cunt is still pulsing with orgasm, fuck me while my body's on come-down and thinks it wants to be left alone—but doesn't really.* It wants to be used; it wants to be an organ of pleasure for him.

"You okay?" he asks, as if he can sense that something's going on in my mind.

"Yeah, I just..."

"What, Maddie? What's up?" He draws his face back from

mine, pushing up on his hands to take his weight off me. *No,* my mind screams, *don't do that, come back, pin me down, squeeze the air out of my lungs and make me feel the weight of you against my rib cage.*

"Nothing, I just...um, I'd kind of banned myself from coming until I manage to keep up my exercise plan for a week."

"What?" His tone has switched from gentle, reassuring, *I know something's on your mind but I want to soothe those thoughts away so I can get on with putting my cock inside you* right through to *What the fuck?* He slides off to the side of me. Not a good sign.

"Don't look at me like that. I thought it would be an incentive, you know."

"How was I supposed to know? I mean, any other time, you'd be complaining if I didn't give you orgasms. Now I'm supposed to not give you orgasms? I want to give you orgasms. Lots and lots of them."

"I know. I know you do. It's me; it's just an idea I've been having."

"Well you'd better tell me all about this idea, so I don't mistakenly make you come again. Hmm?"

"I'd rather you just fucked me now and I'll tell you afterward."

"I've gone a bit soft."

"I could suck it." Surely he won't resist such an offer. I'm gripped by an overwhelming desire to fill my mouth with his cock and feel it hardening into my throat. I start to shift myself around so I can shimmy down the bed.

"No, tell me now," he says. "And what's with this bloody exercise plan anyway?"

I can tell I'm not going to squirm out of this, if he can turn down a blow job until I've explained. "I just, I've been feeling kind of horny lately and..."

"You have?"

"And if you're going to keep interrupting me then I'm not going to tell you anything."

"Yes, ma'am."

I glare at him for a moment. "So, I've been feeling kind of horny a lot of the time..." I can tell he wants to make some smart comment but he holds it back. "And it got me thinking how it feels to be desperate for sex but not able to have it. Like when you're out, or at work or something. And I started to think about having to wait to have an orgasm—but being kept turned on all the time so I desperately want it. You could send me sexy texts and when we're together you could tease me and touch me but stop before I come."

I pause. I haven't really finished, but I'm thinking I should let this sink in.

"Am I allowed to speak now?"

"Yes."

"I like the idea of keeping you all hot and bothered. But I want to make you come. And what the hell's it all got to do with your exercise plan?"

"Oh that. I just know I probably won't stick to it, even though I really want to. When I was out running the other day, I was, er, aroused, a bit, but I decided I wouldn't let myself come until I'd done the gym and a swim this week too."

"And you haven't been for a swim, have you?"

"No. I was going to go in the morning."

"Well, you are a naughty girl then, aren't you? You could have confessed and asked for a spanking. I'm always happy to help you see the error of your ways."

I smile. "I know, but that's not really punishment, is it?"

"No," he laughs.

"Do you understand what I'm saying? Can we try this?"

"So you're not to come for another week, and even then only if you've done all your exercise?"

"That's right."

"But you want me to tease you and keep you aroused all the time?"

"Yes."

"What about me? What if I want to fuck you?"

"You have to fuck me. Whenever you want to. Just don't do it so that I come. Shouldn't be too difficult for you." I wink. Penetrative orgasms aren't really a thing for me. "You should use me for your pleasure as much as you want to, however you want to. Please."

"You realize what this would sound like if I'd suggested it to you? If I'd said: 'Madeleine, I'm banning you from coming unless you get your exercise, but I'm going to use you for my pleasure as much as I like.'"

"Huh, yeah. I'd probably throw something at you."

"But since you ask so nicely, I guess I could manage it. In fact, I think I'll start now."

He's hard again, it seems. Surprise, surprise. He climbs back on and I part my legs. The tip of his cock glides easily down my wet folds to find my pussy and nudges its way inside, making my mouth fall open and a little gasp escape my throat. I wish now I had ignored his request for an explanation and just sucked him anyway. I want his cock in my mouth before I get it in my pussy. I want to lavish it with attention, worship it. Corny, I know. Too late anyway.

"I think you should wear that little thong thing today," he says the next morning as I'm rooting through my underwear drawer. I've slept naked. His idea. PJs banned for the week so he can get to me whenever he wants.

"But it creeps up my ass," I say.

"Yeah, I remember you saying. And I remember you saying that sometimes you liked it."

"Oh, well, sometimes."

"Put it on."

I had no idea he'd have remembered such a thing. So it's day one of the week, Sunday, and I spend the day out with a couple of friends in town with the G-string in my crack thinking about anal, while he texts me things like this: *Imagine my tongue running up your ass then circling your hole, pushing against your muscles, softening you up.*

It's certainly distracting.

Then he has the bright idea on Monday that I should wear no knickers but a tight pair of skinny jeans, since the theater I work at is a casual, arty sort of place. That damn seam. Fuck. He even orders me to go for a half-hour walk at lunch. I spend the afternoon mentally begging him to fuck me hard that night. And he does—after I've been for a run.

I plan to get some exercise every other day or so, but the next day, after he's spent all day texting me things like *Perhaps we should get a chastity belt. A proper metal one you can be locked into for weeks on end, with it pressing hard against you but no chance of you getting to your clit*, he says, "I think you should go on the exercise bike tonight. Naked." And so I go into the basement, strip and ride five miles with that damn seat pressing against me, getting more and more slippery by the second. And then he fucks me right there, bent over it.

"So are you missing giving me orgasms?" I ask him on Wednesday, day four, after a post-work gym session in which I spent the whole time thinking about Lewis's tongue on my clit.

"Hmm," he says, rather than "yes," which is the answer he really ought to have given. He goes on. "Yes and no. I love seeing you come, of course. But knowing that you want it constantly, that you're willing me to fuck you at any time...well, I could get used to that."

And he does apply his tongue to my clit that night, just

enough to drive me to the edge of insanity before he pulls away and fucks me. "Lewis," I say afterward, "I really need to come. I'm not sure I can hold out for the whole week. And I have exercised three times, if you count the bike."

My voice is small. It wants him to say, "No," and stop that whisper that says I could just quietly see to myself; he'd never know.

"No," he says. "You can wait the full week, like you said. And if you make yourself come, it'll be a fortnight next time."

Is it wrong that I want to make myself come in order to earn that punishment? Fourteen days of madness.

On day five, I suck his cock more conscientiously than I think I ever have before. It's all about him. I'm not waiting for my turn; I'm not doing a good job for the reciprocal benefits. I just want to give him more pleasure than he's ever felt. And I really enjoy it. I mean, I always have liked giving head, but this time I *really* enjoy it as if I'm finding new erogenous zones all over my tongue and in my throat. As I do it, he urges my hips around so he can reach my pussy and lazily finger me, slip-sliding in my wetness, stretching me open, but this time carefully avoiding any contact with my throbbing, hungry clit. Still, it tingles as his fingers pull at that skin so close by.

On day six, Friday, I go for my swim before work and as I stare at the bottom of the pool in front crawl I imagine myself a mermaid, with a tail instead of legs and no pussy at all, the maddening desire all there but no physical parts with which to sate it. I'm strangely drawn to the idea. That night as Lewis sits on the edge of the bed getting undressed, I give in to an unexpected urge to kneel down on the floor and rest my head on his leg, like some kind of well-trained puppy.

I don't even suggest that since I've now had my swim too, and it's virtually the weekend already, we could break the seven-day rule.

"I'm not going to fuck you tonight," Lewis says, looking down at me. "I'm going to make you wait for that too, now."

I climb into bed and my hands find their way down my belly all of their own accord, sliding down the insides of my thighs, so close. My fingers dip into my sensitive skin and to my own torment I find I can't drag them away from so near to my clit.

"Er, Maddie, what do you think you're doing?"

"I can't help it. It's driving me mad."

And so he takes one of my belts and does it up tight around my waist and I wonder what he will do next. Is he improvising a chastity belt? No, he's tying my wrists to it with one of my silk scarves so I can't reach my pussy.

"You can't leave me like this all night," I say.

"Why not?" he asks.

"You just, I don't know, you just…"

"See, there's no reason why I can't."

I might as well own up to my disappointment. "I thought you were going to tie something between my legs as a makeshift chastity belt," I say, in a voice that's deeper than any voice I thought I had.

He leans down and kisses me, tucking the sheets around my shoulders. "Go to sleep. I'll try that next time."

Next time?

I don't sleep all that well. I know he'd undo my wrists if I woke him up and asked. But they're not the biggest issue—that's the throbbing between my legs. And the fact that I spend most of the night trying to decide whether I'd prefer him to make me come first thing and get it over with, or whether I could stand some more hands-on teasing for the day if he makes me wait.

I'm awake first, but as I hear him stir, I close my eyes and pretend to be asleep. He slips his fingers over my hip and in between my legs and I squirm and moan and pretend that his touch is waking me and it's his touch that is making me wet instead of the lack of touch I've suffered all week.

"So, Maddie, you've gone a week without an orgasm. And you've stuck to your exercise plan. What do you think I should do about that? Should I make you come now or should I make you wait some more?"

And, lying there with my arms tied to my sides, it seems like the most natural thing in the world to say, after the slightest of pauses, "Make me wait some more, please."

So we go out to the farmers' market, me with that damn thong on again, its stickiness washed out only to get all messy again. *He knows*, I think, as I ask the charming young man at the Lakeland Lamb stall for some chops. *She knows*, I think as I pay for apples and pears at another stall. My cheeks flush.

"No one knows," Lewis whispers in my ear. "No one knows you're so desperate for sex you'd strip off for me right here."

We go for lunch in a cozy cafe and I'm almost certain my wetness must be seeping out onto the wooden chair, but I'm imagining it. I'm not imagining my lost appetite though. Even after viewing the display case of gateaux and meringues and muffins, all I can think about is cock.

"How much do you want it?" Lewis asks me, before running his tongue up the split in a sticky bun to lick up all the cream.

Normally, I'd snigger, but the arousal has quashed my sense of humor.

"Too much. I'm going to explode."

"I suppose I'd better get you home then."

In the bedroom, I pull off my clothes in seconds, but suddenly I feel bashful. I stand there with my hands cupped over my mound. Lewis is still unbuttoning his shirt so it takes a few seconds before he notices my strange pose. "What are you waiting for?" he asks.

"I feel all weird," I say, not knowing how to put it into words.

Instead, I kneel in front of him, undo his fly and pull his cock free. I form my mouth around its head, but Lewis pulls back.

"Why don't you get into bed and let me get my mouth onto you? It's definitely your turn."

I give him a few sucks to help win him over before telling him why. "Um, do you think we could try another week?"

"What? You mean come now and then another week, or..."

"No, I don't want to come."

"You don't...but...you've been waiting all week to come."

"I know. But it's made me feel different somehow. I feel all warm and fuzzy. I want to carry on." I'm utterly failing to explain myself. Lewis sits on the bed and again I find myself kneeling beside him with my head on his thigh as if it's the most natural place for me to be. That's my explanation. Not words, but the small gesture of nuzzling my nose into the fur of his crotch. I know there are labels for it, labels I would never have applied to myself—after all, who's in charge of all this? It's not like Lewis has banned me from coming. No, I've done that myself.

"Okay," he says slowly. "I can't pretend to understand why right now, but I'll try to if you can help me out a bit."

"I'll try to," I say, and smile. Just before I put my mouth around his semierect cock again, some more words tumble out, all by themselves. "I want one of those chastity belts you mentioned too."

# RUTHLESS

## Claire de Winter

He leads her by the hand through the loud crowd to the dart-board where two young guys in flannels and beanies eye them. She settles on a bar stool to the side. He takes the darts out of his interior jacket pocket, and the young guys nod at him.

"We're almost done, man, and then you're up," one of the young guys yells over the din.

He leans down to whisper in her ear so she can hear him over the crowd. "The usual?"

Things are rarely usual with him. She wonders what he's up to.

She assembles her darts, a slim barrel and the flights that made her laugh. A gift from him, they have her zodiac sign on them. Then she shakes out his heavy hammerheads and does the same, his flights emblazoned with RUTHLESS in red.

The young guys finish their game, clean the chalkboard and move aside. She takes her place at the toe-line for a few practice throws, aware of the guys watching to see if she's any good. She throws a twenty, an outer bull, and the third hits far.

He's not back; it's three deep at the bar.

The young guys move closer

"You play in a league?" the one in a beanie asks.

"No," she says. "I just like it. Do you guys have a league?"

They wear stubble and shaggy hair, aiming for a world-weary lumberjack or seasoned steelworker look. They're all roving eyes and the one in the plaid shirt hovers, blatantly staring at her chest. Beanie is checking out the ring finger on her left hand, his shoulders sagging a little when he sees the sparkle. She catches him doing it.

"I can't imagine you boys have much of a problem in a place like this." She smiles at him. They both are really quite attractive.

"I'm sorry?" The busted one sputters into his drink.

Plaid flannel steps forward. "It's men, not boys. And yeah, we do just fine."

"I bet you do," she says, holding his eye. He's handsome, taller than her with lots of dark thick hair and light eyes; she can't see the color exactly. She's thinking if only she were younger, if only she weren't...

He returns then with their drinks—beer in the bottle for him, Jack with lime and a lot of ice for her.

He looks at the young guys, eyebrows lifted, as if to ask *Is there anything else?* On cue, they smile at her and scram just slowly enough to save their dignity, approaching a group of women drinking near the jukebox.

"Oh, they liked you," he says in a low voice as she hands him his darts.

"Nah," she says. "They were just amazed I can throw."

"I watched the whole thing," he says, coming behind her. "They looked mesmerized. Then again, you mesmerize everyone," he teases with a little squeeze of her waist.

She laughs at his cheesiness. "No distracting the player, now," she says, stepping away from him.

They have rules about this since he is notoriously handsy as well as a punk cheater, using any distractions he can to win.

She throws—closest to the bull goes first—and it's looking good for her. He throws farther out, and it's settled. She'll go first for cricket.

She starts strong, a twenty, a double seventeen and a nineteen. They play slop. It's supposed to be fun, after all. She racks her throws, and when she comes back behind the toe-line he asks, "Do you think they're handsome?"

She smiles. Handsome is the word for him—tall and strong, shaved bald and serious with his sleeves rolled up, veiny forearms on display. The guys look young and virile, she'll give them that, lush and fun. "They're cute," she says.

"Kiss of death," he says with a satisfied little smile and throws. His first two hit on target, but his third hits the seven. He racks his points and turns to catch her blatantly checking out his ass.

"Hot?" he asks as he comes up next to her.

"Always with the fishing for compliments." She shakes her head in mock despair.

He takes a swig of beer, his Adam's apple moving up and down. "Always, but I mean them." He tilts the bottle toward the pair who quickly avert their eyes, busted again.

"I suppose so." She takes a small sip of whiskey, glancing over to them to see the one in the beanie smile shyly. Even she has to admit that they've been watching her.

After a few more rounds, he's effectively tied with her.

"You're not on your game tonight," he says. "I usually can't get this close. Distracted by your admirers?"

"Hardly," she scoffs, but it's true she feels them both watching her. It's taken her mind to a different place.

"I'll tell you what," he says. "Let's get you focused. A little wager."

His bets are a running joke between them. He always loses, so he proposes terms that he likes, the last bet being that if he lost he had to eat her pussy on demand for a week. He was purposefully throwing darts into the cork paneling behind the board with a crazy grin on his face the whole game.

She laughs now. "Terms?"

"If you win, I have to make you come twice tonight before we get home." She smiles at that, as he loves getting her off. He's inventive and must have something in mind. Her admirers have spurred him to claim her. "If I win, you have to tell me a fantasy."

She's surprised he'd put something he likes so much out of reach. He loves to hear her fantasies, wheedles them out until she finally confesses. It's only in the last year or so that he's really gotten her to talk about some of her baser thoughts. The ones she doesn't even examine herself. She doesn't often lose, but perhaps tonight he's feeling lucky.

She kisses him, deeply and inappropriately for a bar full of people. "You're on."

She throws a triple sixteen that she's needed and another for points. "Don't want you hauling me off to the bathroom for a hand job now."

"Like I'd drag you into some filthy bar bathroom."

"Wouldn't be the first time."

"And who said it would be my hand?" This raises shivers down her neck; she really does love his mouth.

She can still feel the boys watching them.

"Your little audience is fascinated," he says. The tension is evident, even from across the room. The word "audience" brings a rush right between her legs.

He leans down and quickly places a small kiss on her neck. "Interesting." He steps back; he can read her so easily. "You just need a bull and a twenty to win."

She takes her place at the line, but at the last moment she throws wild. Deliberately.

He turns and beams at her. "You *want* to tell me. You delicious little perv."

He doesn't throw again, just gathers their darts into the front pocket of his jeans. "Let's go." And then they're walking through the crowd and out the bar. She turns to cast one last look at the boys, to see if they're watching. In fact when their eyes meet, flannel turns as if to follow and beanie gives her a small shy wave. And then she's gone.

He's speeding through the streets to their house, clutching her hand and bringing it to his mouth for a periodic kiss. She can tell he's thrilled he won't have to pry a secret out of her. This time it's something given willingly.

When they're home, he drags her by the hand inside, leading her up the stairs.

"Spill," he says when he gets to their bedroom, already tugging at the neck of his T-shirt, taking it off in one swift motion.

Like any of the times they've talked about this, she finds it difficult to look at him when she says it. But he can be ruthless when it comes to her pleasure. So she gets her courage up; if she won't trust him, who will she trust?

"That they're watching."

"The guys in the bar? While we're fucking?"

She nods. "While I'm riding you."

"Mmmm, yes please." He stands in front of her.

"And they, they can't stand it. They're jerking it while they're watching us."

"I love it. An education."

"Yeah."

"Come here." He takes her hands and places them on his belt buckle. His kiss is rough and sloppy and turned on, like he's been every time she's mentioned her desires.

He spins her to hold her in front of him, his chest to her back, like an offering, his fingers work the knot on the side of her black wrap dress, and then she's free. He peels the dress off to reveal her skimpy black see-through panties and a matching black bra that barely conceals her nipples as it pushes her breasts together, giving her ample cleavage.

"See?" he says, addressing their image in the mirror, though he's really talking to the invisible guests in the room. "I know what you guys like." He reaches a hand around to skim the cups of the bra and tweak her nipple, making her blush. "Nice tits, glorious hips; bet you boys have never seen anything like this before, have you?"

She's never felt so fully on display, or so silly. She laughs.

"Nice," he says, walking away. She's afraid she's upset him, that they're done. He rummages in the dresser and comes back with the black silk sash they've used before. "Might help," he says. "Do you want to try?"

She nods, and he ties it around her eyes, adjusting the knot so it's firm but not too tight.

"I know you can see if you want," he whispers. "But try not to, okay?"

She nods.

"And go there with me," he says more quietly.

He turns her and then his chest is to her back again. He fumbles in his pocket behind her as he talks.

"She's a bit shy, my wife. I know you boys understand." He removes something from his pocket and then she feels a sharp point at her throat, which focuses her. "If you want a woman like this in your life, you have to know how to take control of her properly. Watch." She feels the point press a little more firmly against her throat and realizes it's the dart. "And learn."

He trails the tip of the dart down to her cleavage. It's pointed, but not sharp, though he's giving it enough pressure that she's sure it'll leave a red line. With the tip of the point he circles one nipple through the lace and then slides the dart up her shoulder and slips her bra strap down her arms.

"Pretty, no?" His voice is above a whisper, and she smiles. "Luscious," he murmurs in a low and earnest way—a word he's never used with her before. She wonders if that is actually how he would describe her to their audience.

He removes her bra, drops it on the floor, the dart circling and then pressing steadily on the tip of her nipple.

"She looks proper, yes? A lady? How hot would it be if she had a piercing right..." He presses a little deeper on the tip of her nipple. The delicious edge of pleasure and pain sends sparks zinging through her body to her pussy. For a moment, she's not sure if he will stop. "Right here." She has never thought about a piercing. He's never mentioned it, but now it's all she can think of. She starts to feel her audience again, a tingle of how intense it would be to bring those guys back to their house for a show. It's something she'd never do, something she probably shouldn't even think about, but she does.

She feels his hand spin the dart so the flight end is against her and with one hand snakes it down her front into her panties. The thin plastic flicking against her clit once, twice and then his bare finger slipping easily inside as he says, "You'd like me to display you, wouldn't you? Show everyone what a treasure I have?" He takes the dart out of her panties, and she imagines the word RUTHLESS glinting. He hooks the dart tip through the flimsy sheer fabric at her hip, jerks up quickly so her panties snap.

"Hope you're both taking notes," he says to their audience.

And the boys are suddenly more real to her in the room. He lowers the scrap of mesh to the floor and she steps out of them.

When he rises he says, "Yes, you can take pictures."

Her face reddens; she sees the guys now getting out their phones. "But no faces. I'll hunt you down if there's anything I don't like."

He whispers in her ear then. "They're very eager to keep going. I think we can trust them."

She nods and his fingers form a V stroking, down once and coming back up to spread her wide. She imagines one of the guys unbuttoning his pants, the other with his phone taking pictures. Then she feels the cool steel point on her outer lips.

"See?" he asks, as if she is a toy for them to learn on. "Beautiful, isn't it?" The point is sharp, clarifying, focusing, but it doesn't hurt. He glides it up and down her lips, maddeningly lightly, as she wills herself to be still. He circles her clit, the point skimming across from side to side. "The most important part, right here. She likes this, but you know what she really likes? She really likes having her clit sucked. If you're going to learn how to properly take care of a woman like this, you need to learn how to do that."

He kneels in front of her then, his hands on either side of her hips, digging his fingers in as if he's testing ripe fruit. He takes one leg and hooks her knee over his shoulder. She puts a hand out to the mirror to steady herself. Then he buries his face between her thighs, sucking her clit in his mouth and earning a gasp. His mouth is oddly cool, but his tongue is skilled and active. One hand ghosts up the back of her thigh to her ass and then she feels him pull her cheeks apart, spreading her wider.

"Let them know you like it," he murmurs.

She throws her head back, tits thrust out, one hand on his smooth head, riding his face, imagining what she must look like to a pair of horny guys. His tongue laps her sensitive nub and slips against her clit. She imagines them watching, jeans unbuttoned, stroking up with sharp tugs and down with gentler strokes. They are keeping rhythm with their hands, their beautiful cocks swollen and hard, wishing they were in his place, desperate to taste her.

She is so close, and she wonders if he will make her come, clenching around nothing, when he slips two fingers inside her and sucks her clit in his mouth. She imagines the guys coming as they watch her, the evidence slick over their hands and down their shafts. It's then that she comes on her husband's fingers.

When he's done licking her as she settles down, he lies down in front of her. Her blindfold is slipping now, but she doesn't mind. He reaches up and pulls it the rest of the way off so she can see him. "Ride me," he says, his glorious cock rising from the valley between his hips, begging for attention.

She straddles him, suddenly blushing at how wantonly turned on she is, at the pretending they've been doing.

"*Now* you're shy?" He grins as he lifts her hips, bringing his tip right to her edge.

To wipe the smile off his face, she grinds down, taking him inside. His head falls back into the floor, tendons tight in his neck.

"Fucking tight and so hot. It's heaven."

"Mmmm." She is sitting on his lap, rolling her hips over him, feeling his cock fill her perfectly. His hands grip her soft, full hips. In complete abandon she has one hand in her hair, the other pinching a nipple.

"They're saying, 'I bet she is.' They're begging for a turn. Should I let them touch you?"

She closes her eyes, thinking of their hands on her while she rides her husband—hands replace hers, tugging and pinching her nipples, fisting her hair with a firm pull, gliding down her stomach to where she and her husband are connected, sliding deliciously up and down his cock and her clit. She grinds against his hand.

"So responsive," he breathes. "But you're mine. They can only look. Look in the mirror and see what they see."

She turns and sees cheeks blushing, hair wild, breasts flushed, nipples pinked, his thick cock pumping in and out of her. She's never felt more desired. She feels the bite of a sharp point on her ass. He's picked up the dart from the floor. He pricks her with it in time with his thrusts, the small pain a bright note to the lush pleasure of his cock. He continues until his rhythm falters in a haze of need. He's pumping fast and gripping her, both of them about to tip over the edge as he's mashing the blunt side of the dart into her hip, the flight crumpled, his word RUTHLESS flush against her skin.

# SUCKER

## Rachel Kramer Bussel

For the first few months we were dating, I thought my boyfriend Carl's favorite sexual activity was getting fucked in the ass; after all, how many times had I put on a strap-on and guided a dildo between his thick, fleshy asscheeks? The sounds he made when I used even a finger back there were music to my ears. It was like I was taking him to another world. But recently I learned that there may be a rival for his top sex spot.

I had just put on the special black panties I wear when I fuck him, the ones with a hole in the front designed to perfectly hold my cock in place. I was taking out said cock—one of the silicone variety—and about to place it inside my panties, when I decided to use a different kind of lube first. "Open up," I said to him. His brown eyes strayed toward mine for a moment before his lips parted and then his eyes shut. No sooner had I placed the toy about an inch into his mouth, resting the tip against his tongue, than he was sucking it fervently, guiding the entire length down his throat. I hardly had to do a thing.

My pulse raced as I observed his cheeks suctioning in and

out, every facial muscle contorted to swallow the cock with the most efficiency. It was more than a matter of pride, or readiness; his mouth, like mine, was practically made for cocksucking. I know it when I see it, and what I was seeing sent my mind spinning. I'd done this with other lovers, but none of the men had ever taken to it so well.

Emboldened, I slid the toy from between his lips. He whimpered. His glazed eyes opened back up, staring at me with the kind of longing that could make even a tough girl like me cry. He didn't have to say a word; he wanted it back in his mouth, where it belonged. No, wait, that's wrong; he *needed* it. I knew the feeling well. One time he said to me, "I think you like having my cock in your mouth more than you do in your pussy," and I couldn't deny it. Cocksucking, oral gratification, being face fucked into oblivion—that's my real sexual orientation.

I'm not sure why it never occurred to me that it could be his too, but seeing my own desire reflected back on his face made me so hot I couldn't stand it. "You want this back in your mouth, you'll have to put that tongue to good use first." I impulsively whipped off the panties and planted myself over his face, too riled up to wait. I usually love teasing him, and even though he makes mock protests, he does too, but this was urgent.

Tears sprang to my eyes as he dove for me with that same urgent hunger, murmuring something into the folds of my pussy as I smashed my knees against his ears. I rocked back and forth as he slid seamlessly along my sex. We thrashed like that, his tongue and lips taking me to the edge of orgasm over and over, but not quite getting there. The image of him with that cock down his throat was as exciting as anything he could do now. What would happen if I found a man to do exactly this, to hover over Carl's face, but instead of his tongue darting out, his throat would open up and swallow a cock, while I watched every thick, hard inch disappear inside the love of my life?

"Yesss," I hissed, the sound almost angry as I once again tore myself apart from him. He didn't make a sound, just watched me with those same hungry eyes. I leaned down to kiss him, his tongue plunging into my mouth, needing to fill a space, needing to connect. I'm a sucker for a man who can admit his mouth is like a pussy when he's turned on, a hole demanding to be stuffed with whatever I choose.

I pulled back, reaching deftly to the bedside table for the dildo. "Remember this?" I asked with a grin, as I balanced one hand against the headboard, while easing the toy inside me with the other. "Jealous?"

"Donna, fuck," he said, his face contorting again. Some guys might ask to touch their cock in this situation, but my Carl, he was beyond the no doubt aching hardness between his legs. We were communing on a different level. He opened his mouth, a wet, moist oval all for me.

"Hold my knees," I commanded, and when he had me secured, I lifted myself so I could keep the toy's head buried as far inside me as it could get it, while shoving my fingers into his mouth. He sucked them fiercely, teeth and tongue tangling, asserting an animalistic kind of dominion. I rocked forward, the toy pressing against new pleasure zones, while twisting my fingers the way I might with my hand inside a sweet, writhing girl. That's the thing about Carl; we can be everything to each other at any moment, him a cockslut one second and a wet cunt the next.

He strained, asking with those stretched lips and sucking motions for more. "You want my whole hand, is that what you're saying? You want to show me how much you can fit in that big mouth?" His hands answered by clamping down even harder on my legs, digging in. I eased my hand out to let him breathe, wiping his wetness across his cheek. "There are so many things I want to do to you, baby. Good thing we have the rest of our lives." I followed up this sappy statement with a slap across the face, grateful he'd shaved so the color showed up bright and vivid.

His eyes brightened, moist with the same desire as the rest of him, followed by a droplet of drool sliding down a corner of his mouth. "Are you wet for me, is that what you're trying to tell me?" I gave him another slap, the sound echoing in the room as I shifted the dildo in and out, my wetness adding to the sexual cacophony.

I pressed my hips down, so aroused the toy felt as if it was expanding like a real cock, as I curled my hand and fed it to him. I wasn't trying to truly get it all in. I didn't need to; it was the thought that counted. Carl grunted, making me slide up and down on the toy even more fiercely. "Take it," I demanded, grateful my small hands, the one truly delicate part of me, were up for the job. Carl made room between those pearly whites for my offering, slobbering all over and making delicious noises.

I was still poised at the ready for my climax, but I needed and wanted him to finish the job. "My turn, then you get your present," I said, pulling the toy out and keeping my gaze locked on his as I licked it from the base to the tip, tasting my tangy juices. I bounded over him, propped myself on my back and let him work the toy back into me while doing whatever he does to my clit that always feels like a rocket's about to go off inside me. I've never been able to duplicate that feeling, even with the finest toys around.

"Donna, you just...that was amazing," he said as he plunged the toy inside me. Somehow it always felt bigger when he did it. "You got me to fit your hand in my mouth."

"I have other plans for you, like a nice hard cock," I said, the image settling over both of us as he made my clit sing. He rotated the toy as I spun out my fantasy. "Maybe I'll fuck your ass, which I know I didn't get to do tonight, while you take some stranger's cock and suck it the way you did to my fingers tonight." His grunt, and the way his fingers picked up an almost inhuman speed, were all the answer I needed. "Oh yeah, I bet you'd like to be filled in both holes, a big dick in your ass and one ramming down your throat, and you not able to come until he does. Or maybe until you swallow it all? I'd have to stop and watch, maybe have him spray it right between your lips."

The image was so clear in my mind; it was almost like it was actually happening. Carl's heavy breathing filled the room once I couldn't talk any longer, only feel. When he flicked his middle finger at my clit, hitting it in precisely the same spot over and over again, I shook, clamping down around the toy as my climax took over. He shifted so his knee could hold the dildo in place while he spread my hood open and slapped at my clit. When his cock brushed against me, I knew he wasn't just giving me the sensation I craved, but taking as well.

I came again, this one making me slam my fists against the bed, straining upward, my entire cunt engaged in the action. When he finally eased the toy out, I was shaken. I'd been on cloud nine, but he'd brought me right back down to earth, practically chained to this bed.

I gave him my most wicked grin, rousing myself from the stupor of afterglow. "You definitely deserve your prize. Put that down and get back to where you were before and close your eyes."

Carl didn't waste a second, and neither did I, slithering back into the panties, which felt snugger as they pressed against my wetness. I eased the dildo inside, gave his cock one sensuous lick for good measure, smiling as I tasted the precome waiting for me at the tip, then straddled him as I'd imagined our anonymous lover doing. Once again, I hovered above him. "Ready?" I didn't really need to ask, of course, but seeing him nod and stick out his tongue was reason enough to do so.

Carl seemed to draw the toy toward his tongue like a magnet, and before I knew it, he had once again taken almost all of it inside him. "I'm going to turn around," I said. I'd been planning to wait, to focus on one sensation at a time, but that taste of him had made delaying impossible. His muffled reply combined with his help spinning me around were all the answer I needed.

While Carl held my hips, I stretched myself across his body to take the head of his cock between my lips. The deeper he took me, the deeper I took him, our mouths and cocks entwined just as our lives were entwined. No, I couldn't literally feel each stroke of his tongue against the toy, but I could feel a corresponding jolt of his flesh against my mouth, his dick pounding like a heartbeat as we fed each other, and fed each other's appetites. That mystery man was a fantasy I'd be happy to revisit, but this was what kept me alive—my Carl, giving every inch of himself to me, shamelessly hungry and needy, open and ready and willing to try anything. I'm a sucker for that.

# APPLE THIGHS

## Jade A. Waters

Cassie plopped down on the bus seat, a puff of air falling from her lips as her thighs slapped the vinyl surface. She shoved her purse against the wall while the vehicle rumbled to life, then gazed down at her legs.

*Apple thighs.* Not thunder thighs. Not thick thighs. *Apple thighs.*

Cassie glanced out the window as the city transit bus pulled away from the therapy complex. She had plenty to work through. Twenty-nine years old and a surprising number of weird experiences to address—but she was plugging away. Kate was a great therapist full of questions, leading her through all the nitty-gritty drama that had made up Cassie's life. It had barely been two months and she was already feeling better. Stronger. Today, she'd brought up the body topics. "My mother still picks on my thighs," she'd said. Understatement of a lifetime right there.

How many times had Cassie heard it growing up? *You're so beautiful, honey. So fit, so lovely. Except for those apple thighs. But don't worry, it's hereditary.* Kate had stared back at her with the widest eyes when she explained this one: round, juicy thighs that tapered like the base of an apple when they reached her knees. Cassie knew her mother adored her. They spent plenty of time together, but it was no secret that body issues ran in their family. Repeatedly, Cassie had talked herself down after this comment, knowing damn well that there was nothing wrong with her thighs and she merely came from a long line of self-conscious women.

But hearing it still set the gears in motion in her head.

The bus hit a pothole, lifting Cassie off the bench for half a second. In the return to the vinyl she felt the spreading out of her thighs, the flesh flattening on the seat beneath her. Maybe if she'd worn a longer skirt or pants, she wouldn't have noticed. Maybe if she didn't have the background she did, she wouldn't think about it. Like all these other people on the bus—thick, thin, tall, short, curvy, straight—a bounty of types, and all of them lovely and going about their business on this bus just like her. To Cassie, all of them were beautiful in their own unique way. Like her thighs. Her round apple thighs that, one day, she'd be proud of. That she should be proud of.

She peered down at her legs. Her skirt was perhaps a little too revealing, but all her jeans were dirty and she had only been going from home to therapy this afternoon. She'd always liked this skirt, though she'd shoved it into the back of her closet after her ex-boyfriend had commented on its length. *"You sure love to flash those big-ass thighs, don't you?"* She blinked away the memory, knowing the statement had no value because he had been an asshole. But in the context of losing a job and having her car break down for the hundredth time this year, it was too easy for it all to come to a head.

Really though, everyone had a type. Everyone had a body. This was hers—apple thighs and all. So she wore a skirt better suited to a nineteen-year-old. Who cared?

Cassie cared. She could talk herself up all she wanted, but in the back of her mind, as confident as she was, she couldn't pretend it didn't sit there like a lead weight, the one flaw that all women were rumored to have and were supposed to get over. This is what she'd mentioned to Kate, knowing that someday, she was going to love these thighs. She was not going to glare at them with the memory of her mother's comments. She was not going to remember her jerk of an ex and his insensitive reference to her "glaring imperfection." She was almost thirty, and that seemed like a damn good time to get over all of this.

Cassie pressed her palms onto her thighs. She'd been blessed with smooth, unblemished skin most of her life, so even stocky as they were, her thighs had the consistent, unmarred fair coloring that covered the rest of her body. As the bus continued its roll down the city streets, the flesh of her thighs shook. She had thin calves and narrow knees, but above them her legs curved out to a substantial width. In truth, she had a lot of muscle in those thighs from years of dancing and running, but they were definitely the outliers from the rest of her body.

She pursed her lips and ran her hands back and forth, grazing her skin. She could rest on her tiptoes to keep her legs up so that her thighs didn't appear so wide, like two sturdy pancakes smashed out on the seat. But she kind of liked the way they looked. They carried her. They made her womanly. Plus, she was able to outrun all the women in her former running group—big, strong apple thighs and all.

Cassie fanned her fingers over her thighs and rubbed her palms along their lengths again, sighing. Her skirt caught on her wrists as she glided her hands up, crumpling it at the top of her thighs. She peeked at the seat across from her. Two older women sat there, the one by the window staring out and the one on the aisle reading a book. They didn't notice her. No one in front of her would see what she was doing, either. She turned her head, checking out the seat behind her at a diagonal. No one there.

But the man behind her cleared his throat.

Cassie flattened her skirt and shoved her hands to her knees, her face burning as she whipped it forward.

*Oh, fuck.*

Had he seen what she was doing, mindlessly stroking her thighs?

More importantly, was she insane, rubbing her thighs like that in public?

As if in answer, the man lifted himself in his seat. Cassie held her breath. The entire bus was frozen in time, the driver watching the road, and the other occupants reading books, listening to iPods, or chattering about the news. But this man slid around the seat and sat beside her, not a word coming from his mouth as he peered forward.

She turned her head slightly, examining him from the corner of her eye and realizing she'd seen this guy before. She'd even smiled at him once, the last time she'd been stuck on this bus. He was handsome, his face peppered with the tiny hairs of one who didn't shave every day, and he had hazel eyes that shimmered thanks to the sun streaming through the window beside her. When she saw him a few days ago, he'd been wearing a baseball cap, but now his sandy blond hair was loose around his ears, making him look a tad older than he once had. Midthirties, late thirties...Cassie wasn't sure. But she could tell that he was some sort of painter, his T-shirt and jeans always speckled with dried paint. Today he wore a spot of fuchsia on his right thumb and a streak of red along his left wrist.

She straightened her head again, her nerves on high. Had he seen what she was doing?

She felt his scrutiny on her then, and a chill fogged her body.

When he spoke, his voice came out a deep bass that prickled her skin.

"Do you mind if I sit here?"

Cassie shook her head, her fingers latched around her knees. Her legs suddenly felt hugely exposed, though she did choose to wear this skirt in public, and apparently had no problem touching her thighs a minute before.

*Idiot.*

"It's a better view," he said.

Cassie bit down on her tongue.

Maybe he meant the window. Or being one seat closer to the front of the bus.

Or maybe she really was an idiot.

"Yeah," she said, her heart racing. "Sunny outside today, isn't it?"

The man raised an eyebrow and smiled. Cassie broke out in goose bumps. She hadn't made an ass of herself on this bus, had she?

She willed herself to look back at him, wondering if her thighs had turned as crimson as her face—because wow, was she blushing, her cheeks burning with embarrassment. The sensation ran the entire length of her body in under a second.

"It is. But that's not what I was talking about." He gazed directly at her thighs, then back to her face. "Please don't stop on my account."

Cassie didn't move.

The man kept grinning at her. She was surprised she didn't find it uncomfortable, or awkward. In fact, she shifted slightly on the bench, keenly aware of how hot it was at the apex of her apple thighs.

"I...uh..."

Cassie pinched her lips together. Great, now she sounded like an idiot, too.

The man scooted forward in the seat, enough to block her from the view of any other passengers. He was tall, and with the muscles in his arms alone, it was clear he was strong beneath his jeans and T-shirt. She could do whatever she wanted right here in this seat, and no one would be the wiser.

Cassie shook herself. Was she actually thinking about this?

The man put both hands on his thighs, then tilted his head toward her legs before dragging his hands in an upward motion.

He was modeling what he wanted from her.

Her stomach knotted but her heart thumped in her ears. His smile was so sweet, so warm. So encouraging.

She slid her hands up her legs, halting them mid-thigh. Her fingers were shaking.

Now the man cupped his thighs, and Cassie did the same.

Beneath her panties, her groin swelled with heat. The flush running through her body was like a teasing caress, and she gripped her thighs again. He met her eyes and nodded.

"May I?" he asked.

He laid his fuchsia-spotted hand on her thigh, shocking Cassie to the core. He didn't move it at all; he simply rested it next to her hand, his fingertips and palm hot against her skin.

Cassie trembled. Beside her hand, his was wide and strong. He had beautiful, long fingers broken only by that spot of fuchsia high on his thumb. It covered his knuckle, the color cracked from repeated movement. She imagined what his fingertips would feel like running all the way up her thighs.

She kept her hand beside his but inched the other one higher. Her thighs were warm. She'd smashed them so tight to the vinyl that they'd surely make a popping sound when she stood. The bus stopped to let more people off, then more people on, but Cassie didn't notice. All she noticed was the sound of her breath, ragged in her throat, and the intense stare the man gave her as he nodded again.

"Please," he whispered.

Cassie couldn't believe how excited she was. She arched her back slightly, letting her pussy rub against the seat. Her skirt had crept up beneath her bottom, and she was pretty sure her panties made direct contact with the vinyl. Somehow, this didn't bother her. She shifted her hand up, the fabric of her skirt gathering at the tops of her thighs.

The man curved his hand across her leg, forming a better grip. He stretched out his fingers, digging the tips in so that they indented the flesh of her thigh—an apple thigh held tight in his grasp. Cassie had dated plenty, but none had spent more time on her thighs than it took to get into her panties. A grope, a slide, then fingers prepping her for a swift fuck.

This man inhaled a heavy gasp as he squeezed her leg again. His skin was dark against her light, his fingers firm to her soft. He hooked his pointer finger around hers, an endearing effort to hold her hand—but he didn't look at her face, instead mesmerized by the appearance of his hand on her thigh.

She didn't look away, either.

The bus swerved, shifting him an inch closer to Cassie. His thigh was practically against hers, and he parted his lips to whisper the same word again.

"Please."

Cassie eased her other hand beneath her skirt.

The man remained still, holding her thigh and her pointer as she pressed the pads of her fingers against her swollen clit. There was a whirlwind of pleasure dancing through her limbs, and when she gave herself a few rubs, she rolled her hips to grind against the seat.

"Yes," he said. He clutched her thigh harder. Cassie shivered as she stroked herself, slipping her fingers beneath the hem of her panties. She was sopping, captivated by the fuchsia speck on his hand and the firm grip of his fingers on her big round thigh. Gently, subtly, she rocked her hips, sneaking her fingers inside her wetness and giving the quietest of whimpers when she pushed them all the way in.

The man stroked her finger and her thigh. Cassie worked her fingers in and out, in and out. The pressure surged in her cunt and she bent her thumb to swipe at her clit again. She clamped her lips shut, fighting the urge to scream, to moan so loud as this man kept squeezing and caressing her thigh—her apple thigh, which suddenly appeared so thick and lovely beneath his hold. It struck Cassie that her thighs formed true curves of woman-hood as she buried her fingers deeper inside, and beside her, the man's breath was almost as loud as hers. When she rolled her pelvis forward again, the swell of ecstasy started to overtake her folds, quaking her insides. Her movements became frenzied as she chased the sensation and he noticed, clenching tighter. Then he leaned toward her face, blowing warm air into her ear. Cassie sank her fingers as far as she could, her body racked with a climax so hard and fast she choked down a wail that surely would have stopped the bus.

They hit another pothole as Cassie struggled to breathe, her body shuddering atop the vinyl seat. When she pulled her fingers free, she kept them tucked beneath her skirt. They were sticky with her excitement. Her gaze locked on the man's hand. He curved it around her thigh, then ran it over her other leg. Finally, he turned it palm up. An offering.

Cassie met his eyes and slid her damp fingers into his grasp.

He smiled, then pressed her hand beneath his, guiding it along her thigh so both of them could caress her flushed skin. Cassie's breath had returned to normal, but her cheeks tingled from her indulgence as the bus rolled up to the curb.

"You have the most delicious thighs I've ever seen," the man murmured.

She gasped as he released her hand and stood. It was his stop, the same one he'd taken the other times she'd seen him on the bus. He winked at Cassie, and as he headed toward the front of the bus, she hoped she'd see him again. He disappeared down the steps, and then passed her window with a wave.

The bus gave a throaty roar as it picked up again, and Cassie stared down at her thighs.

They were her beautiful, luscious, apple thighs, and she wouldn't wish them away for the world.

# LITTLE GIRL BLUE

## Laila Blake

It'll be fun," she said. "A great way to meet new people, people like you. It's for charity," Tara added. Her eyes glinted darkly and she bit her lip. Tara's a switch, and I'm not. It's how she wins arguments, every time.

And now I'm kneeling on a padded pedestal in the club she manages and my thighs are shaking under the strain. I'm not the only one; there are eleven of us, liberally sprinkled across the room, like living statues, like dolls in a giant's playhouse. All of us are naked under long capes. The hoods shadow our faces, and simple, unadorned masks obscure our identities even more. We are color-coded—my cape is blue, marking me as free, but trained. I don't think it was meant to be humiliating, but to me, it sets me apart as a slave someone grew tired of. Once upon a time. I shiver and press my palms onto my thighs, willing warmth to spread through my flesh.

A thin metal chain connects my collar with the wooden lectern beside me. There are only two names on the clipboard it holds, two small bids. Both, I think, are pity bids. At least it's almost over; they announced it earlier. We're in the last half hour of bidding.

*It would be fun*, Tara said. She's standing across the room in black leather, looking fabulous and schmoozing some of the richer patrons of this establishment into more and more exorbitant donations.

*A great way to meet new people, people like you.* I watch Tara; it passes the time. I try to remember that by daylight and out in the real world, we aren't so different. We both love British period dramas and we like to take walks by the marina. She manages a club and I run a small animal shelter. But in here, she's gorgeous and confident, and she exudes the kind of magnetism that sets her apart, even among this exclusive clientele.

I'm not glamorous like the patrons, like the other slaves for auction. It doesn't matter that we all wear the same thing, that the mask hides the lines that have just started to appear around my eyes this year. It shines through; it's in the way I hold my body, in the lack of tone or tan. I don't know.

I'm just a girl who's almost thirty, and somehow the last few years passed me by in a haze of work and books, friends and concerts. I don't belong here. This is not a place for me to meet new people, *people like me.* I'm submissive, I will always be submissive—that doesn't mean I have anything else in common with any of them.

"Reveal, slave," a stern female voice says to my left. A shock runs through my body and I snap my gaze back to the floor where it belongs. Then I swish the sides of the cape over my shoulders. I suck a silent breath through my teeth and stare at the hardwood slabs, slightly discolored from shoes trampling around all evening. The mask obscures my vision to a degree, but I can see her in the corner of my eye: an elegant woman in a slinky long evening dress, standing next to a man.

She sighs, tapping the leather pad of a small strap against the hollow of her palm. They are not allowed to touch, not before they've purchased one of us for the evening. Even then, it's not a given—that was stressed several times.

"You slouch, slave," she informs me tersely, then chuckles as I adjust my posture. "Better. Are you sure blue is your color?"

"Oh Lena, don't tease the merchandise," the man next to her says, shaking his head. He steps closer, so close I can almost feel his body heat up the air between us. His eyes follow the contours of my breasts and the curve up my shoulders.

"I forgot," she says, folding her arms across her chest as she inspects my bidding sheet. "You have a thing for rejects and broken things. Quite an eccentricity, my dear."

He makes a noncommittal sound and tilts his head, his gaze still upon me. I close my eyes under the mask and try to breathe. My cheeks are on fire, and submissive or no, I want to slap her. Or more accurately, a far more courageous and impulsive version of myself does. Suddenly, though, a different feeling emerges, layers over humiliation and anger, and I squirm to try to relieve the aching sensation down between my legs. He is still watching.

"Stand, slave," the woman called Lena says then. She's picked up my bidding sheet and is playing with the pen. My jaw trembles as I rise to my feet.

"You want her?" she asks. I push my legs apart and fold my hands around my elbows behind my back. It's been a while, but even amid all this humiliation and playacting, I have pride enough to show I still know how a slave moves, which positions to assume.

The man doesn't say anything.

"Have her. It's on me. Don't worry, she won't go for very much."

"I can pay for my own slaves, Lena, thank you. Give me that."

I can't see her, but I want to think she flinched at the sound of his voice. I did. And a hot shiver ran down my spine. I sway, seized by a sudden sense of vertigo.

She says something; I don't hear it, but her heels click loudly on the hardwood floors when she walks off to inspect the other slaves. I swallow hard; I can't see him, but I don't think he's left. It doesn't feel like he has.

"You may cover yourself again, slave."

His voice comes from my side, but I manage to keep looking straight ahead as I pull the sides of the cape back over my shoulders. It doesn't close in front of me, but it hides my nipples and lends at least a little bit of warmth.

"What's your name?"

I clear my throat, bite my lip. He's not supposed to ask that, but I think he knows.

"Elise, Sir."

"That's a pretty name."

"Thank you, Sir."

I can hear him playing with the clipboard, reading through my limits and kinks. Quite in spite of myself, I feel my heart rate pick up, a little at first and then hard enough to make my voice pulsing and throaty.

"How long since you were last owned?"

I hesitate, lick my lips, and then stare at the floor around my feet. "Five...five years, Sir," I whisper despondently.

He hums once. But just as I am quite sure he is about to move on, I hear the scratchy sound of pen on paper. I hold my breath, dare to watch him sign his name to my bidding sheet. I can't read it, but his hands are large and strong. In a flash of mental acrobatics my brain supplies images of these fingers in my cunt, in my ass, closing around my throat.

"It would be a pleasure to win you, Elise," he says. Then he looks up. For a second or so, our eyes meet. They are blue, dark blue, in a complicated face all angles and sharp planes, lines and bone. I shiver; he sets the clipboard down and turns away.

"Thank you, Sir," I say when I catch my breath. He pauses, but doesn't turn around. I watch the back of his neck and the sweep of his shoulders until he disappears from view.

The final shuffling begins soon after; the hall erupts in movement. All of us are told to kneel again, to keep our eyes on the ground. I am jittery and nervous, and not a small part of me is getting tired of the rigid role-play, the overwhelming displays of power whenever a group of dominants get together.

Finally, someone comes around and collects the different clipboards. I hold myself steady, try to keep breathing as I watch their shoes appear and disappear from view.

One by one, the winning bids are announced. One by one, the leashes are unclipped from their lecterns and handed to the winners. The woman, Lena, takes hold of a pretty slave girl, blonde and perky and barely twenty-one. She fetched the highest price that evening, Tara tells the crowd, but when the girl looks at her Mistress for the night, a flicker of fear replaces the pride she felt just a moment ago.

I swallow hard and look away. My heart is pulsing in my neck, my temples, and the crowd moves on to the next slave, a young man, shaved head to toe, and wearing the blood-red cape that marks him as trained and owned. He's been sporting an enormous erection almost all evening and looks faint and needy. The Master who claims him, though, does not give the impression that he'll take pity on him anytime soon.

Then it's my turn, and I can't breathe. Tara gives me a secret kind of smile, but it doesn't help.

"Slave number five," she proclaims as she consults his clipboard, goes for three hundred dollars to Sir"—she pauses for dramatic effect—"Jonathan."

I dare to look up, and he steps forward out of the crowd.

It's him, with the dark eyes and the complicated face. I shiver, suddenly so far more nervous than I could have expected to be. I want to be anywhere but here, I want to be at home with a book, where it's safe.

Instead, Tara unclips my leash and hands it to my new owner in exchange for a crisp check. *I'm a whore*, I think. *I'm a piece of meat, and not only that but my friend is watching, facilitating the sale.* All that shouldn't make my clit tingle so hard I can hardly concentrate on the clapping and the noise, but it does. A large hand wraps itself around my chin.

He has a grip like a vise as he forces my face up to look at him. He looms high above me as I kneel on the low pedestal. Behind him, the crowd is moving on. It's only his eyes now that are roaming over my face. My cheeks feel warm under the mask.

"Follow me," he says, his voice barely rising over a growling murmur. He allows me a moment to get to my feet and then, leash jangling between us, he leads me out of the large communal hall into a private playroom. Tara showed me these once, while I visited during the day. It was funny then; now I can hardly breathe with nerves.

He picks up a blanket, puts it around my shoulder and then directs me to sit on a low bench he has dragged closer to the bed. I assume it is usually in place for spectators, but we are alone; he closed the door behind us. I clutch the blanket around me, mostly for warmth, but also for modesty and a minute sense of safety. He sits down maybe two or three feet away from me on the bed. It's covered in crimson linens and still looks freshly made.

"Are you cold?" he asks. I look down at the blanket and shake my head.

"It's already...getting better."

"Thirsty?"

This time I nod, a little guiltily. He doesn't seem to mind, though. He gets up and leaves the room. I close my eyes and try not to faint. It seems like no time at all until he comes back with a glass of orange juice. I gulp it down fast.

All too soon, I'm clutching the empty glass. He is still looking at me.

"Are you nervous?"

"I...I've never done anything like this before," I admit, words tumbling from my mouth faster than I can stop them. "Um...Sir." The truth is, I haven't submitted to anyone in years. I had to practice kneeling at home for weeks in preparation of the evening. That almost tumbles out after the rest, but I just manage to close my mouth before it does.

He nods though, hardly moving at all.

"I thought not," he says quietly. "That's why I bid on you. I haven't either. A friend dragged me along; I don't think you liked her very much." A crooked smile crosses his face. "Didn't think I'd take part in the night's festivities, to be honest."

I lick my lips, and then finally manage to look up at his eyes again. There's a dark blue storm brewing in them; it's hypnotizing.

"Thank you, Sir," I whisper, "for...for the drink."

He shakes his head, but takes the empty glass from me, then sets it on a table by the wall. When he comes back, he stops behind me. Slowly, his hands descend onto my shoulders. I feel their warmth, their strength, all the way through the blanket.

"But I did buy you, slave," he whispers as though I hadn't interrupted his train of thought. His breath stirs the little fluff in the shell of my ear and a shiver runs down my spine. He takes hold of the blanket and slowly eases it off my shoulders. "Stand and show me what I bought."

I hold my breath, letting the dizzying sense of vertigo travel through my body. It makes my toes tingle and I wriggle them against the plush carpet. I lick my lips, and then stand. My fingers shake as I try to open the cape where it's tied at my neck. Finally, the knot gives. I push the hood off my head and the cape flutters to the ground behind me.

I can hear Jonathan breathing on my back. He picks up the cape and blanket and stashes them out of reach. I squeeze my eyes shut under the mask and slowly push my arms back until I can wrap my palms around my elbows. My muscles protest at this; I try not to grunt at the effort. This, too, I had to practice again.

"Turn around, slave."

I've always thought that any nerve-wracking situation is eased and softened by someone telling me what to do. Jonathan's commands are quietly uttered, without malice, but without any room to disagree, either. That makes it easier when I turn and present my naked body. The metal leash still hangs down from my collar, runs between my breasts and pools on the floor. That's where I direct my gaze, but like before, he clamps his hand around my chin and forces me to look at him.

"I want to see your eyes, slave. Don't look at the floor unless I tell you to. Understand?"

"Yes, Sir," I confirm tremulously. I keep my gaze on his face as he steps back again to look me over. I can see his eyes sweep over my breasts down to my stomach and my freshly shaved cunt. He takes his time while the blood sloshes loud in my ears, a constant stream of white noise and vertigo.

"Interlock your hands behind your head and spread your legs a little further." It's like my body reacts to his external command, bypassing my decision center completely. "Further than that. *Wider*. Yes, good. Good girl."

I can feel air brushing against my labia, against the slippery wetness between them. He makes me spread my legs until they drag my labia open with them, until I feel the strain of standing this way. Then he lowers himself to the ground, squatting there as he looks up at me. He smiles once, then lets his gaze travel down my stomach and tilts his head to inspect my cunt. My thighs are shaking now. I press my eyes shut until he stands again and I remember his earlier command.

"I am told that I may only touch what I bought if you consent, slave," he says slowly. His eyes seem to pierce into mine even through the small holes of the mask. I hold my breath. "Do you consent?"

I gasp for air, try to speak but my glottis feels pasted shut. Finally, I give up and nod instead. He clicks his tongue.

"I'm going to need more than that, girl. Take off that mask and speak up."

Unclasping my fingers, I reach for the elastic and pull it out from under my hair. The mask falls away in my hand. It's only now that I feel truly naked, and a shiver runs through me.

"I...I consent, Sir," I say shakily.

"To what, girl?" he goes on, taking the mask from me. He tosses it onto the table where he put my cape earlier. "Just to being touched, or to being used in any way I see fit?"

There is a power in humiliation, like electric charges, and I have almost forgotten how deep it reaches inside of me, how fully it takes hold. I nod, lick my lips. Since I took off the mask, my hands have been hanging at my sides, and I don't know what to do with them. In this one moment, it's almost as though the last few years of being alone never happened, like his hands are reaching into the deepest, darkest part of me and have already laid claim to it, far before he ever asked me for consent. Anything other than total submission would be a lie—to myself, to him, to the promise my eyes gave him half an hour ago when he inspected me on the pedestal.

"The latter, Sir," I whisper, forcing my eyes to stay on his as he told me, even though every instinct inside tries to drag them back to the ground.

"Say it."

"I consent to being used, Sir, in any way you see fit."

He nods, just once. Nothing changes. Then everything changes, like sudden static in the air that crackles in my hair. I hold my breath and he takes a step closer.

Without warning, his hand—that strong, large hand with a grip like a vise—disappears between my legs. I gasp, and he grabs hold of my cunt like it's a new toy he just acquired.

"You're sopping wet," he rasps. His cheek brushes over my temple; my breath comes in hard, pressurized spouts. "Is it because I bought you like a little whore? You liked that?"

I nod, blindly, helplessly, as he slips two fingers inside me and a groan escapes my lips.

"Answer me."

"Y-yes, Sir. I...yes, I think so, that's part of...yes, Sir."

He hums, driving his fingers into me so hard I have to rise to my toes with each stroke. I lean my head onto his shoulder, trying not to collapse on my shaking knees as I keen a moan against his shirt every time he pushes into me.

And then he stops, so abruptly that my head is reeling, trying to catch up. I stare at him, eyes wide and dilated as he brings his fingers up to my face. He paints my juices onto my lips, under my nose. Then he turns them around and spreads what's left on his knuckles over my cheeks. I smell of cunt; my face is burning.

"Be a good little whore and clean them, girl."

He barely gives me time enough to open my mouth before his fingers invade it hard and fast. I gag once, and then I can get myself under control and start suckling, swishing my tongue and lapping up every last taste of me.

He pats my head, humming his approval; I glow under his praise. After maybe a minute of this, he smoothly moves into finger-fucking my mouth. He leans in closer, so close that I can feel his lips move against the shell of my ear while I splutter and choke under the onslaught.

"I'm not going to fuck you tonight. I'm not going to fuck you for charity. Do you understand?"

I try to nod even though I am not sure I do.

"If I fuck you as my whore, I will pay my whore. And if I fuck you as my slave, then I'll fuck you if and when you've earned it."

Again I nod. He pulls his fingers from my mouth, and then rests the wet pads of his fore and middle fingers against my lips. His teeth graze along my neck, sending shooting spasms down my spine. I wriggle my toes and my hands to release the tension.

"On your knees, girl."

He offers a steadying hand as I sink to the floor, eyes huge and needy as I look up at him. Already this is easier, like a line of memory he is slowly replacing with his own. I open my mouth in some instinct to plead; already I want little more than to be bent over that bed and fucked long and hard, forced to take it any way he wants, fucked until he replaces the memory of emptiness. But he doesn't and I don't dare request it.

"You are going to watch me, girl," he growls, pulling down the zip of his pants and unpacking his cock. He is hard and big, more in girth than length, and it makes me shudder, cross-eyed with longing. He has the kind of distinct mushroom head that plugs into you hard and fast, that can invade orifices and lay claim to them with a single stretching stroke.

His hand encircles his shaft and he starts to pump, lazily at first as he watches my face fall.

"Hands behind your head again," he grunts, breathing a little harder already. I obey, as though if I just heed him fast enough, he'll change his mind and let me have a taste of him after all. Instead, his hand starts to pump faster.

"Why have you been without a Master for so long?"

I look up, surprised, cheeks reddening even more—quite involuntarily. I swallow hard, try to gather my faculties enough to speak.

"I...I was shell-shocked at first, I don't know. Getting over my ex." I suck a sharp breath between my teeth; again I have to force myself not to look away. "Then I just...I don't know. Maybe I was scared to risk it again. Or...I don't know, Sir."

He nods.

"And you don't submit to strangers." It's not a question, but I nod anyway, even though my current condition seems to prove me a liar. But he seems to understand.

"But you miss it." Another grunting statement, again not a question. It's obvious from my reaction, I think, and I exhale a shaking breath. Quite in spite of myself, my eyes fill with tears as I nod.

"Yes, Sir."

"You ache for it." Every word comes out hard and fast, a sort of staccato sound with each stroke of his cock. "Crave it. You're hollow without it."

Again I nod, and the first tear runs down my cheek. That's the moment when he groans and splatters his come all over my face. It lands in the corner of my eye and on my cheek, on my nose and my lips.

"Fuck, you're pretty when you cry," he whispers, bracing himself against the bedpost behind me. Almost gently, he uses his cock to wipe another drop of come into my hair. He sniffs, runs a hand through his hair and then stuffs his softening cock back into his boxers. I bite my lip to stop a keening sound of longing from escaping my throat.

I think he's long read it in my eyes, anyway.

From his pocket, he produces a business card, and I lower my hands to take it. It says he runs a business called Leather-Works. I shudder with a pleasant sense of fear.

"You won't wash your face tonight. You won't touch yourself. And tomorrow you may call me, and maybe we'll arrange something new."

I stare at him, and then back at the card. I nod, cradling it in my hands like a treasure.

"Answer me, slave."

"Yes, Sir." I whisper, "I will call you tomorrow."

"With my come still on your face."

"Yes, Sir. With your come still on my face."

"That's a good girl…Elise."

# DO ROBOTS BREATHE?

## Tamsin Flowers

The man on the doorstep looked exactly as if he'd stepped from the pages of the Robo-Lolly catalogue. He was dressed in a crisp, tight uniform of palest blue serge and even wore the same little bellboy hat that the man wore in the catalogue, complete with the red starburst logo. And when Tilly looked at his face, she realized it *was* the man from the catalogue—the same very handsome man with his brown eyes and chiseled features. Smiling at her. Standing on her doorstep holding a large pale-blue box, tied with a navy-blue ribbon.

"Are you Tilly Mattila?" he said, maintaining his megawatt smile as he spoke.

"I am," said Tilly.

"Then this is for you," he said. "From Robo-Lolly. Would you like me to bring it inside?"

"Yes, please," said Tilly, holding her front door open wider and wondering how she could inveigle him to stay for a while.

He didn't wait for instructions but marched straight through to Tilly's small, sunny kitchen and placed the box on the table.

"Thank you," said Tilly, coming through behind him.

"My pleasure," said the man, executing a deep bow with a flourish of his arm. Then he was gone, pulling the front door shut behind him, before Tilly could think of anything else to say.

Left alone, she went over to the kitchen table and looked at the box. There was a label, on a pale-blue card, naturally, hanging from the navy ribbon. On one side it read *Deliver to Tilly Mattila* in old-fashioned cursive script. No address details, simply her name. On the other side it read *PEN15* in the same handwriting. Not for one moment, when she'd applied to Robo-Lolly to be a product tester, did she think she'd be selected—but obviously she had been. However, she couldn't remember from the catalogue what the PEN15 was. She'd been hoping to get the automated outside window-cleaning robot, to save herself from a chore she hated, but she knew that was the WINCO42.

"So just open the box and you'll find out," she said out loud to herself, feeling the same little buzz of excitement that she got on Christmas morning or her birthday. She pulled on the end of the navy ribbon to undo the bow and then lifted the lid of the box and put it to one side. The first thing she pulled out was a thick, parchment envelope with her name on the outside. She ripped it open and withdrew a letter, handwritten, on the same thick paper. But she was too excited to read it and dropped it onto the lid of the box. It was far more important to find out what Robo-Lolly had actually sent.

All she could see in the box was a tangled nest of bright-red shredded paper. She plunged her hands in and felt cold metal— not altogether unexpected, given where it had come from. She took hold and drew the object out of the box, scattering a cloud of red confetti across the table and onto the floor. It was heavy and solid for its size. She shoved the box backward off the table and set her treasure down in its place, blowing away the remaining shredded paper as she did.

Tilly blinked. The PEN15 was a small silver robot, realistically styled as a miniature man, about two feet tall, wearing the pale-blue Robo-Lolly suit and hat, complete in every detail right down to the starburst logo in miniature. Despite his chrome complexion, he looked just like the man from the catalogue, the man who'd delivered the box to her less than ten minutes ago.

What would the little man do for her?

She picked him up again to examine him more closely, looking for an ON-OFF switch to make him work. She turned him first one way and then the other but there was no indication of what he would do, no buttons or dials, even when she felt up under the back of his jacket with her finger. But she did notice that his metallic skin was now warm. She could have sworn he was cold to the touch when she took him out of the box.

She put him back on the table and sat down opposite him. She remembered the letter.

Dear Tilly,

Thank you for offering to test one of our products—we are so very grateful to you and would appreciate your feedback on the enclosed form.

Sincerely yours,
Robo-Lolly

That was it. No explanation, no instructions. Tilly wondered what to do next and absentmindedly picked up the feedback form. There was one question and a large empty box, presumably for her answer.

*Did PEN15 completely satisfy you?*

No, thought Tilly. Not remotely.

"Do you want to play, Tilly?" said the robot.

Tilly gasped and looked around to see if someone else had come into the room. No, it was just her and the PEN15. And that meant...the damn thing just spoke to her. And it knew her name.

"What?" she said. She must have imagined it.

"Do you want to play, Tilly?" he said again.

Tilly blinked and then laughed.

"Yes."

"Good." The PEN15's voice was not the least electronic. In fact, it sounded like the catalogue man's real voice. Perhaps it was. "Please follow my instructions exactly. First, take me to your bedroom."

Tilly's eyebrows shot up but she decided to play along with whatever the game might be. She picked up the little man and carried him up the stairs to her room. He weighed about the same as a human baby.

"Do you have a name?" she said.

As she put him down on the bed, he bent quite naturally into a sitting position.

"My official name is PEN15," he said. "But I'd like it if you gave me a pet name."

"Okay. What about PEN for short?"

"That's very nice," said PEN15. "Undress me."

With trembling fingers Tilly slowly unbuttoned the little blue jacket and pulled it off over his shoulders. The robot's arms moved to make it easier for her. He seemed, quite gradually, to be coming to life. He wore nothing under the jacket so Tilly was able to gaze at his impressive chrome pecs and six-pack straight off.

"And my pants," he said.

"Yes, sir," said Tilly, not sure whether to laugh or simply comply.

"You can call me 'sir,' if it makes you more comfortable."

"I'll stick with PEN," she said, undoing the press stud that fastened the pale-blue trousers. *Will he have a cock?* she wondered. She had to presume so, given the turn the game seemed to be taking. But when she pushed his pants down she discovered nothing but a rounded chrome bulge between his legs.

"Now you," said PEN.

"Me what?"

"Undress," he said. "You agreed to play my game."

If Tilly wasn't mistaken, he sounded a little petulant. That's all she needed—a spoiled child of a sex robot.

"Take your clothes off and join me on the bed."

Tilly tried not to snigger as she pulled off her yellow sundress and the pink matching underwear she wore underneath it. She stood naked by the side of the bed, suddenly self-conscious. *Don't be stupid*, she told herself. *He's just a toy.*

PEN15 patted the coverlet next to where he was sitting. Tilly sat down. She felt anything but relaxed and emphatically not turned on. But as she sunk down on the bed, she became aware first of a whiff of men's cologne and then of the heat rising off PEN15's small body. She took a deep breath.

"You like it?" said PEN. "I chose it this morning with you in mind."

"But you don't know me."

"I chose you, Tilly Mattila, from all the applications to test Robo-Lolly products. There were thousands and I chose you. Now, lie back, please, and close your eyes."

This made Tilly feel a little nervous. What exactly was going to happen next? Was he going to dry-hump her with the silver bulge between his legs? She lay down on the full length on the bed, resting her head on the pillow, and closed her eyes.

"That's better," said PEN.

A hand touched the outer edge of Tilly's thigh. A warm,

flesh-and-blood human hand, not a steel robot hand. Her eyes sprang open and she sat bolt upright, looking around. But it was just her and PEN, alone in the room.

"Who's there?"

"Sorry," said PEN. "That was me. I didn't mean to surprise you."

"But…" Would it be rude to say it? "You're made of metal. That felt…real."

"Lie back and close your eyes, Tilly. Our testers all agree that it's the best way to experience it."

"What, exactly?" said Tilly.

"I'm beginning to wonder if I made a mistake choosing you, Tilly."

A robot with attitude?

"Okay, okay."

Tilly lay back down and closed her eyes again. When she felt the brush of a hand on her rib cage, she squeezed her eyes shut tight and bit her lip. It seemed incredible that a metal robot could have such a warm, human touch. The hand moved to her breast, cupping it in a way that seemed impossible for the size of it. It truly felt as if she was being fondled by a full-sized man. Real fingers brushed the tip of her nipple, scattering a volley of little shocks down through her body. She was starting to feel turned on, even though she didn't understand what was happening.

"How do you do it? How does this work?" she said, eyes still shut as the warm fingers traced a path down her stomach.

"Shh, Tilly. Just lie back and relax while I do my duty."

Duty? Tilly liked that. She flung her arms above her head on the pillow and surrendered herself to the sensations now flooding through her. This had to be better than the WINCO42. PEN meanwhile had reached the vortex between her legs and was softly exploring. Tilly sighed as he gently slid a finger up between her lips.

"You're wet, Tilly," he whispered. "Well done."

His words made her stomach flutter. Was she really starting to feel desire for a robot sex toy? She felt PEN's weight shifting on the bed and she sensed that he was now positioned between her legs.

"I think I know what you'd like, Tilly," he said.

Oh. My. God. The PEN15 had a tongue and, boy, did he know how to use it. Tilly loved nothing more in the world than a man going down on her—and she would have quite happily sworn that no sex toy on earth could truly replicate the sensation of an eager tongue orchestrating her climax. But she'd been wrong. PEN started slowly with long, slow strokes of his tongue along the outer edges of her lips. Then she felt it burrow in between them, pushing inside her, hot and rasping. She could even feel PEN's breath—do robots breathe?—warm and moist against her pussy. Although PEN was small, his tongue was anything but. She felt it wiggling up inside her, constantly moving, building friction against her G-spot, and she started to writhe against it as deep sighs rolled up from her throat.

PEN's tongue pulsed and pumped into her, soft and mobile, prodding against her most sensitive spot until Tilly moaned and gasped with pleasure. But the sex robot had hardly started. Slowly, so slowly that Tilly wanted to scream, he withdrew it from deep inside her and started caressing the soft folds of flesh that swathed her clit. His tongue worked gently to slide them open, to splay them wide just as he pushed her legs farther apart with authoritative hands. Tilly's knuckles were white on the headboard and she was chewing down hard on her bottom lip, trying to contain the small whimpers she was emitting with every pass of PEN's tongue. Her hips pushed up toward him but it wasn't as if he needed any guidance on what to do next.

He sucked her engorged clit into his chrome mouth but all Tilly could feel was the softest pressure of lips and tongue, the tantalizing sensation of suction and the enticing nip of teeth against yielding flesh. She wanted to come, she needed to come… but every time she reached the edge, PEN seemed to sense it and scaled imperceptibly back, keeping her trembling on the brink, willing to fall but held *in situ*. Her heels beat the mattress and her hips bucked.

"PEN," she cried. "PEN, let me go, let me have it."

The little robot ignored her and carried on with what he was doing with a level of skill that Tilly had never encountered in life or even in her wildest imaginings. Only when she was primed to the point of sobbing distraction did he finally relent, using his tongue to jettison her into climactic orbit. At the same time, he pushed fingers—Tilly was in no state to work out or even care how many—up inside her, giving her muscles something to work against as they contracted again and again while she threw back her head and gave vent to all the pent-up frustration and longed-for sexual release that she hadn't even realized she was carrying inside her.

But still the artificial tongue continued to work, dancing in circles around her clit, the lips pursing and sucking, the teeth nibbling deliciously. Tilly spun somewhere in the stratosphere, undulating in the waves of her orgasm. Just pure sensation.

Eventually PEN brought her back down to earth. Tilly sighed and opened her eyes.

"Not yet, Tilly," said PEN. "We're not finished."

Tilly obediently closed her eyes again, despite the fact she felt completely spent. Surely he couldn't do any more to her? She waited, breathing deeply to recover herself, listening to see if she could work out what PEN was up to. But there was nothing—he was completely silent.

"PEN?"

"I'm here," said the little man, and it was astounding how much Tilly felt comforted by the sound of his voice. "Just waiting for your heartbeat to come back down to normal before we carry on."

"Oh," said Tilly, a little nonplussed.

PEN stroked her arm.

"Nearly there," he said.

A minute passed and Tilly wondered if she was going to fall asleep. But then she heard a soft whirring beside her.

"What...?"

PEN stopped her from speaking with a long, deep kiss on the mouth and Tilly felt herself surrendering again. Then, as his lips broke from hers, he took one of her hands in his. She let him guide it and was rewarded with the touch of something warm and hard with a velvety surface. She grasped it, her hand only just able to encircle its girth.

"Oh, PEN," she whispered. "Is this yours?"

"I think I'm the only guy in the room," he said. "Don't you?"

Robot sex with humor. Could things get any better?

She slid her hand up and down the length of PEN's cock.

"Can you feel that, PEN?" she said.

"Yes," he said. "I was manufactured with sensory, pressure and temperature receptors all over my body."

She gripped tighter and moved her hand up and down more quickly.

"Does it feel good?"

Pen made a sound like a cough and then spoke in a slightly higher voice.

"My receptors simply record data, Tilly. As a robot, I don't experience either pleasure or pain. I'm here to indulge you with whatever pleasure or pain you desire."

"So if I give you a blow job, you'll never come?"

"I've been programmed to approximate orgasm if required."

Tilly laughed and rolled onto her side, pulling PEN toward her by his cock. When he was close enough, she leaned forward and planted her lips on its domed end. She quickly found the small slit with her tongue and the whole organ felt so realistic that she wondered if she were dreaming. She sucked the cock into her mouth but it was almost too big, stretching her jaw and making it difficult to breathe. PEN's hands came around to support the back of her head and she began to slowly move backward and forward, pulling the cock in deeper each time until her jaw started to click. She held it tight at the base and under her palm it throbbed and twitched so realistically that she put her other hand underneath to see if PEN had balls. Of course he did. The most extraordinary creation. She wondered how Robo-Lolly had manufactured him—but not for long. The task in hand took all her concentration. She wanted to see the little toy come.

His grunting sounded realistic enough, and his panting. She could feel the pulse of a vein at the base of his cock and as she worked it, it became hotter in her hand. Inside her mouth it felt like a one-hundred-percent-real, living human man dick. But it tasted better than any she'd ever come across and she couldn't get enough of it, sucking it in, grazing it with her teeth as she pushed it farther and farther back toward her throat. She wanted to taste his come like nothing she'd ever wanted before and she didn't let up, relishing in the response she could feel under his skin and grunting in her ears.

"Come on, baby," she whispered against its shaft. "Come for me."

With a long moan the PEN15 came. Tilly felt his balls constricting in her hand and then a stream of hot, sweet fluid jetted out of the end of his cock and filled her mouth. It was delicious, delightfully flavored like salty vanilla caramel. Tilly swallowed a mouthful and carried on sucking, pumping him with her hand for more of his nectar until finally it receded to just a tiny dribble.

"Oh, PEN," she said. "That was delicious. Was it good for you?"

"The earth moved, Tilly."

"You are a glorious thing, truly," she said, lying back satisfied against her pillows.

"I'm afraid the product test isn't over until I've fucked you," said PEN. "Please ready yourself for the finale."

"I'm ready."

Tilly braced herself to receive the monster cock where it was designed to go. She kept her eyes closed and she spread her legs wide. She could feel PEN moving on the bed and a second later she felt his hands settle on the inside of her thighs.

"You have a beautiful anatomy, Tilly," said PEN, "especially here." Fingers stroked across the outside of her pussy and she felt a rush of heat. "Are you wet for me or shall I lube you up? Let me check." A finger slipped inside her and Tilly's back arched as a burst of pleasure spiraled through her.

"You're wet," said PEN. "I thought you would be. You're a very sexual creature, Tilly. I like that about you."

Tilly had high expectations and PEN didn't disappoint. His cock brushed along the line of her labia and then slipped softly inside like a thief in the night. But once in, Tilly could feel it growing, stretching and lengthening, becoming if anything larger than it had been inside her mouth. The walls of her pussy expanded to accommodate it but as PEN started to thrust backward and forward the fit became tighter and tighter, until the friction worked up to a burning sensation inside.

Tilly gasped. The combination of pain and pleasure went perfectly together, like sweet and salty popcorn, sending ripples of delight through her body. PEN pumped harder and faster, faster and harder; pain and pleasure seared and burned her until she wouldn't have been surprised to see smoke rising from between her legs. She gasped and grunted, mewling as the little robot with the monster cock gave her the fucking of a lifetime.

"Oh, PEN," she sobbed, "oh, PEN, I'm going to...I'm going to...I'm coming. I'm coming."

After that the words were drowned out and she felt as if she was being turned inside out, tumbling over and over herself, with only one fixed point in her universe—the hard thrust of the robot cock inside her, just managing to anchor her and stop her spinning away out of control.

"Oh, PEN..."

"How much do you cost?" said Tilly, as they lay side by side, wet with Tilly's sweat, on the rumpled bed.

"Tilly, you must know that I'm very expensive. This was a free product test but I don't think you could afford to buy me."

"Oh."

Tilly closed her eyes. She didn't want to package PEN back up in the pale-blue box with the red shredded paper and hand him over to catalogue man to take away.

"How much, PEN?"

The figure PEN gave was almost what Tilly earned in a year as a shoe store manager.

"But Robo-Lolly offers installment plans, don't they?"

Tilly knew they did. She'd been reading the Robo-Lolly catalogue for years.

"Yes. Would you like one?"

Tilly nodded her head and heard the sound of rustling paper.

"Sign here," said PEN, "and fill out your bank details."

Ten minutes later the agreement was sealed in an envelope and waiting on the hall table for catalogue man to collect it.

"Now, PEN, remind exactly what it was you did earlier with your tongue," said Tilly.

She lay back among the pillows and closed her eyes. Oh, yes, the PEN15 was definitely better than a WINCO42.

# ABOUT THE AUTHORS

**M. BIRDS** is the author of "Sparks" which appeared in *This Is the Way the World Ends*. She writes and makes films in Vancouver, British Columbia.

**ELIZABETH BLACK**'s erotic fiction has been published by Xcite Books (UK), House Of Erotica (UK), Circlet Press, Ravenous Romance, *Scarlet Magazine* (UK), and other publishers. She lives on the Massachusetts coast with her husband, son and four cats. Parts of *"Babes"* appear in her novel *No Restraint* (Xcite Books).

**LAILA BLAKE** is an author, linguist and translator. She writes character-driven love stories, cohosts the podcast *Lilt* and blogs about writing, feminism and society. Her body of work encompasses literary erotica, romance, and speculative fiction. She lives in Cologne, Germany with her cat Nookie, loves obscure folksingers and plays the guitar.

**CLAIRE DE WINTER** is a novelist and recovering attorney. Her erotica has appeared in numerous anthologies. She lives in the industrial Midwest with her husband and their family.

**LAUREN MARIE FLEMING** (laurenmariefleming.com) takes the guilty out of pleasure. Author of *Bawdy Love: 10 Steps to Profoundly Loving Your Body*, Lauren speaks at conferences and colleges, teaches interactive workshops, and hosts intimate retreats all around the world.

With stories in more than forty anthologies, **TAMSIN FLOWERS** (tamsinflowers.com) has probably been writing erotica for far too long, but she isn't going to stop. Having completed her year-long *Alchemy xii* BDSM novella series, she's now turning her attention to a new novel of a dark and twisty hue.

**DENA HANKINS** (denahankins.net) writes aboard her boat, wherever she has sailed it. After eight years as a sex educator, she started writing erotica and romances spanning the queer alphabet. *Blue Water Dreams* and *Heart of the Liliko'i* are erotic romance novels with queer and trans leads.

**DARSIE HEMINGWAY** landed in the wild Pacific Northwest after waving farewell to a litany of lovers in New York City. She now holes up in a tree house writing literary erotica and inventing places where she can be free to do anything and everything she dreams.

**TILLY HUNTER** (tillyhuntererotica.blogspot.co.uk) is a British erotica writer with a wicked imagination and a fondness for tales of ordinary folk discovering their kinks. She has had numerous stories published by the likes of Cleis Press, House of Erotica, Storm Moon Press, MLR Press and others.

**MALIN JAMES** is a writer with a book fetish. Her work has appeared in numerous magazines and anthologies, including *Best Women's Erotica 2015, Mutha Magazine* and *Bust*, as well as various podcasts. She is currently working on a short story collection.

**REGINA KAMMER** (kammerotica.com) writes erotica and historical erotic romance. She has been published by Cleis Press, Go Deeper Press, Ellora's Cave and her own imprint, Viridium Press. She began writing historical fiction during NaNoWriMo 2006, switching to erotica when all her characters suddenly demanded to have sex.

**D. L. KING** (dlkingerotica.blogspot.com) is the editor of anthologies such as *Carnal Machines* (IPPY gold medal winner), *Under Her Thumb* and *The Big Book of Domination* (both IPPY silver medalists). Her stories can be found in *Slave Girls, Bound for Trouble, Hungry for More* and *Fast Girls*, among many others.

**ANNABETH LEONG**'s (annabethleong.blogspot.com) work has appeared in more than thirty anthologies, including *Best Bondage Erotica 2013* and *2014, Can't Get Enough* and *Bound for Trouble*. She writes erotic novels for Ellora's Cave, Breathless Press and Sweetmeats Press.

**SOMMER MARSDEN** (sommermarsden.blogspot.com) is a professional dirty-word writer, gluten-free baker, sock addict, fat wiener dog walker and expert procrastinator. Called "one of the top storytellers in the erotic genre" by Violet Blue, Sommer's the author of numerous erotic novels including *Lost in You, Restricted Release, Restless Spirit* and *The Accidental Cougar*.

**REI PARDIEU** (thoughtsofagrowingsub.tumblr.com) is a UK-based BDSM blogger with a love for sex toys and erotic fiction. She also adores cats, anime and spending time messing around on Tumblr. This is her first erotic publication but she hopes to write more.

**OLEANDER PLUME** (oleanderplume.blogspot.com) writes erotica in several genres. Her work can be found in *The Women Who Love to Love Gay Romance* edited by Ryan Field, *Best Women's Erotica 2014* edited by Violet Blue and *Take This Man* edited by Neil Plakcy.

**HEDONIST SIX** is an author of erotic romance based in London. Nobody's perfect, neither are her characters, which makes them all the more relatable and well-liked by her fans. Reviewers have described her debut novel *Just Another Day at the Office* as heartfelt and unique within the genre.

Editor, writer, American *desi* and lifelong geek **SULEIKHA SNYDER** (suleikhasnyder.com) published her first short story in 2011. Subsequent releases include three Samhain Publishing novellas and short stories in Cleis Press's *Suite Encounters* and *The Big Book of Orgasms* anthologies.

**JADE A. WATERS** (jadeawaters.com) once convinced a boyfriend that the sexiest form of foreplay was reading provocative synonyms from a thesaurus. She's been penning erotic tales in California ever since. Her latest works are included in *Best Women's Erotica 2014* and *The Big Book of Submission*, both from Cleis Press.

# ABOUT
# THE EDITOR

**RACHEL KRAMER BUSSEL** (rachelkramerbussel.com) is a New Jersey–based author, editor, blogger and writing instructor. She has edited over sixty books of erotica, including *Best Women's Erotica of the Year, Volume 1; Come Again: Sex Toy Erotica; Dirty Dates: Erotic Fantasies for Couples; Hungry for More; The Big Book of Orgasms; The Big Book of Submission; Lust in Latex; Anything for You: Erotica for Kinky Couples; Baby Got Back: Anal Erotica; Going Down; Irresistible; Gotta Have It; Obsessed; Women in Lust; Surrender; Orgasmic; Cheeky Spanking Stories; Bottoms Up; Spanked: Red-Cheeked Erotica; Fast Girls; Do Not Disturb; Suite Encounters; Going Down; Tasting Him; Tasting Her; Please, Sir; Please, Ma'am; He's on Top; She's on Top; Crossdressing* and five volumes of *Best Bondage Erotica*. Her anthologies have won eight IPPY (Independent Publisher) Awards, and *Surrender* won the National Leather Association Samois Anthology Award. Her work has been published in over one hundred anthologies, including *Best American Erotica 2004* and *2006*. She wrote the popular "Lusty Lady" column for the *Village Voice*.

Rachel has written for *AVN, Bust,* cleansheets.com, *Cosmopolitan, Curve,* The Daily Beast, elle.com, thefrisky.com, *Glamour,* Gothamist, *Harper's Bazaar,* Huffington Post, *Inked, Marie Claire,* Mediabistro, *Newsday, New York Post, New York Observer, The New York Times, O: The Oprah Magazine, Penthouse,* The Root, Salon, *San Francisco Chronicle,* Slate, time.com, *Time Out New York, The Washington Post,* and *Zink,* among others. She has appeared on *The Gayle King Show, The Martha Stewart Show, The Berman and Berman Show,* NY1 and Showtime's *Family Business*. She hosted the popular In the Flesh Erotic Reading Series, featuring readers from Susie Bright to Zane, and speaks at conferences, does readings and teaches erotic writing workshops across the country and online at LitReactor and her site eroticawriting101.com. She blogs at lustylady.blogspot.com.